BLOODY FOOTPRINTS IN THE SNOW

DECLAN BURNETT

SEVERED PRESS
HOBART TASMANIA

BLOODY FOOTPRINTS IN THE SNOW

Copyright © 2021 DECLAN BURNETT

WWW.SEVEREDPRESS.COM

ISBN: 978-1-922551-72-6

1

The four men strolled out of the Brink's warehouse, each shouldering a very heavy black duffle bag; casual, as if they weren't in the midst of the kind of heist crime families pass down from generation to generation. They wore police uniforms and kept their heads downturned for the cameras lining the property and beyond. A white panel van was parked on the street only feet from tall, razor-wired gates. Once the men dressed as cops got to within ten feet, the side door of the van slid open and two more men—also dressed as cops—shoved two little girls and a woman out. Their hands were zip-tied and duct tape covered their mouths.

Overhead, three crows watched the action until the spinning tires of the van sent a stone pinging off the chain-link fence around the Brink's lot, banking perilously close to the birds on the hydro line.

The teary trio—the girls and their mother—hurried toward the building, silently praying the man inside the facility was okay. Those men in the van had forced him to open up and make the money available. If he wasn't okay, the girls would be without their daddy and the woman would be without her husband.

The van was already several miles from the scene when their description lit the airways of the police band radio. It did nothing to lessen the fabulous mood of the six men because they'd planned for a quicker response and, thusly, had scads of time to get to where they needed to be.

Nine miles from the Brink's facility, the six men climbed out of the van—an electric Ram with self-driving capabilities—and lugged the €800,000,000 in cash to another Ram van awaiting them. They piled in and headed into the woodlands north of the city. Thirteen minutes later, this second self-driving van was rolling away from the vast stretch of open field where one of the six had paid a farmer a reasonable sum to use the property as an airstrip. The farmer didn't ask questions and accepted the money—times were tough. What the men did on the plane wasn't the farmer's business.

The men climbed into the 1986 Cessna 206 Stationair plane with the payload. The plan was for Chauncey, a man who'd logged more than 30,000 hours flying in his long life, to pilot the plane through the mountains, out of the country, shaking any potential trouble from the authorities, and land far on the other side. The final four members of their team awaited them in the frosty climes beyond. Once they landed, they'd each take their share and ride off into the sunset.

The air was clear, but crisp at that altitude. The plane bolted over the bumpy field and took to the air smoothly. Chauncey glanced over his shoulder to give a thumbs up to his counterparts. They were all grinning, and the man furthest to the back slid a white and red Coleman cooler along the carpeted floor. The lid flipped open and he retrieved the first of two bottles of Dom Pérignon. He handed out glasses from the same cooler and then the bottle, which was empty by the time it made a single round. The men sipped and imagined their futures with all that cheddar. What they'd done was remarkable, and they'd managed not to kill anyone, though they were prepared to do so. For that kind of money, you had to be prepared to do so.

Chauncey turned to give another thumbs up to the guys—he had the plane approaching the final set of peaks—when the man at the back popped the cork on the second bottle, but did so with the grace of a toddler on ice skates. The projectile cork slammed into Chauncey's throat. None of the others noticed and the plane slowly began losing altitude while Chauncey gasped and faded while he clawed at his neck.

By the time any of the men noticed, it was too late. The nose of the Cessna clipped a snowy peak and the front of the plane crumpled all the way back to the cockpit. The men made wide-eyed faces and the dash alerts pulsed like the world's loudest digital clock. The plane dipped to the right and that wing tore away, taking with it two of the rear seats. One duffle bag tumbled free, and then a second. The man who'd been in charge of the cooler died instantly when a chunk of steel slipped sideways through the hull like a deftly thrown Ninja star. One man remained screaming until the Cessna thumped so hard into the snow that his head rattled and he broke four molars when his jaws snapped together.

The survivor came to with a start. His face was so cold it hurt, but he only noticed that for a moment before the agonies of surviving a plane crash took the pole position of his thoughts. He felt to his lap and found the frosted seatbelt coupler. He tipped out of his seat and looked toward the cockpit. It had become a crepe with bloody man as its filling. He saw most of the money and sighed.

They'd planned for this. If the plane had to go down to avoid detection, a GPS beacon would give away their location, but only to those who knew the signal. All he had to do was wait and survive the cold.

"Anybody else...?" he trailed. He was a lone survivor and that made him sick, until he considered the sum of his new cut. "Shame," he said then, though was smiling with the left side of his face. The right side was bruised and seriously swollen.

He crawled over the remains of one of the guys—he couldn't tell who and was too shaken to recall the seating plan—and into the snow. He looked around. Breathtaking. A million miles from anywhere. Snow and mountain peaks as far as the eye could see.

He needed a fire, first and foremost, and then he'd have to do an inventory. He'd survive this if he kept his wits.

He stomped to the rear of the plane. The wing was gone and a large hole promised doing an inventory would be a short and sour task. He reached in and began tearing at the broken seats. He then heard footfalls coming upon him, and coming fast. He spun, sending up a white plume of powdery snow.

The thing was huge and its incredibly cold hands were on either side of his face. His eyes clued in immediately to what he saw, but didn't believe it, which really didn't matter. Those hands—paws?—squeezed the sides of his head together until he thought he could taste his brain at the back of his sinus. He opened his mouth to say the single word that danced on his tongue, but his skull cracked and that was it for him.

He didn't even get the chance to say *yeti*.

2

"Must be a pretty nice assignment, huh?" the hotel concierge said from behind the huge marble check-in desk and his computer monitor.

The four men who'd signed into Le Sommet as being with Gabriel Environment Surveying all smiled at this, though none of those smiles seemed totally authentic. As if they simply wore the smiles to meet what might be expected of them.

"Right, the checkout day is in a week. I have you in four separate rooms, in a cluster. Will there be anything else?" The young man's eyes sparkled, banking the reflected flashes from the crystals hanging down from the ceiling.

"Yes. Where do we find Raphael Le Page?" Sidney Fortina asked. He was in his early forties and a little soft around the belly beneath his ski jacket.

"Mr. Le Page can usually be found at the pro shop, but…" the concierge trailed as he typed on the keyboard and scrolled with the mouse, "ah, he will be through with his current lesson at the top of the hour, if he sticks to his posted schedule, and…" he scrolled some more, "it appears he has nothing else booked."

"Pro shop, where's that?" Maurice Lazar asked. Fifty-two but looking sixty by modern standards, Maurice was trim, but built strongly and seemed an ill-fit for his ski jacket and high boots.

"Pro shop, it's through the mezzanine, at the

foot of Petite Colline; that's the beginners' hill, where the main chairlift will take you to any of the hills." The concierge slipped four small envelopes housing key cards onto the desk counter.

"I thought the chairlift was, like, in some rooms or something," Dusty Volpe said. He was rotund with curly black hair and pockmarks rutting his cheeks that really accentuated his passage into middle age.

The concierge smiled. "Only the penthouse suites have private access to covered chairlifts." He then leaned in. "It keeps anyone from snapping video of an A-lister looking silly as they exit a lift, which is rarely, rarely done gracefully."

"All right, I'll ask," the fourth man said after a woman in a parka with a fluffy hood came by his side and began tugging his sleeve and whispering into his ear. "Is the Ice Capades every night or, you know, special?"

The concierge brightened. "It's every Tuesday, Thursday, and Sunday of the season. My partner's in the show."

"So, uh, what time's that at?" Riccardo Gillaspie, the fourth man, was tall and broad. He had very large hands and eyebrows as thick and fuzzy as caterpillars.

"Six PM. Here are your keys. The Wi-Fi is unsecured so you don't need a passcode. If you need a secure connection, one can be made available for a small surcharge. Thank you for choosing Le Sommet. Enjoy your stay." The concierge gave a winning smile and held it until the un-doctor-like scientists stepped from the check-in desk.

The woman who'd joined them turned back and said, "Hey, there any dancing done here?" This was Sofia Spinnel and if anybody asked, she was a lab assistant—in reality, she was Riccardo's fiancé and more than he could handle; she was only twenty-six and acted eighteen most of the time.

"Thursdays through Saturdays in the discoteque," the concierge said and then, because he didn't buy it anymore—maybe before they'd all spoken and revealed their mannerisms—he added, "Good luck with all the *research*."

"Sure, yeah," Sofia said and clacked her heeled boots quickly to catch the guys at the elevator before it went up.

"Scientists…good grief, why do you bother?" the concierge said and then the phone on his desk began ringing and he answered, "Bonjour, Le Sommet."

3

Raphael Le Page loomed large over the five-foot-two Kammie Kassion. The American socialite had rented his services every day for the past week and had finally made it clear that she wanted him to join her in her room. As beautiful as she was, and perfectly sculpted, he was forty and wasn't about to taint the weather at his place of employment. He'd been an Olympian in his twenties, but the sport was biathlon, which did not translate into big endorsements—no Wheaties, no Remington, no Nike, no Head—or lucrative opportunities before, during, or after all the pomp and circumstance of the competitions had cleared. He needed this job and he'd seen countless staff—mostly servers—fired for sleeping with famous guests.

"Is this right? I feel like I'm not bending far enough," Kammie said and squatted her genetically engineered rump while looking back at Raphael. "Can you do the thing again? I'm all off center."

Raphael exhaled slowly and pushed off, skiing up behand Kammie and putting his hands on her hips. She pressed her ass against his manhood and he groaned inwardly.

"It's like I can only really keep steady with your hands there," she said and laughed.

They were on a private kitty-hill and had been for most of the instructions.

"Your hands are so big and reassuring, I don't know…I'm just not learning very quickly, am I?"

she said.

"I think…" She turned her ski some so he was pushed harder against her. "I think you'd do all right with a little more speed."

"Do you really think—" she started and then curved her right ski too hard without adjusting her left ski and sent them down into a slow heap. She managed to get herself turned mid-fall so that when Raphael landed on her, they'd be face-to-face.

"Are you okay?" he said, trying to rise.

Kammie held him tight and licked her plump— but not too plump—lips. "What's the rush?"

"Oh, I—"

Kammie silenced him, pressing her lips against his. He let it go on, even let his tongue graze her tongue and his hand play up the curve where her butt and leg met, but forced himself to stop it there.

"That was nice," she hummed.

Raphael leaned close to her ear. "Would you believe me if I told you I'd do anything you asked?"

"Would you believe me if I told you I'd let you do anything you wanted?" she volleyed.

"You're killing me," he said and then lifted himself so he was no longer on top of her. "And I'm sorry. If things were different—look, Le Sommet fires anyone they discover fucking the guests."

"We'd better not get caught then," she said.

He huffed. Her voice was like candy. Her lips were like candy. Her curves were like candy. And he suddenly had a tooth so sweet it ached, but no.

"We won't get caught, because—"

Kammie rubbed the front of his snow pants. "We'd only get caught if I made another tape and we leaked it to—"

Raphael thought of the video with her and that singer and had to press his face to the snow to regain himself. "I'm sorry, but I can't." He pushed her hand away.

She smiled then and kissed his cheek. "Nobody's said no to me in a very long time, not for sex anyway. You have no idea how much fun it's been with you, actually doing the deed might've ruined it—though, goddammit, you make me hot— so, thank you, Mr. Le Page." She then kissed his lips again, little more than a peck.

He rolled onto his side. Kammie got up to her feet, and hopped to the ski that had popped from her boot. She reconnected and grabbed her poles.

"I know it's fruitless, but you know where to find me; I leave in the morning," she said and then skied away with the deft motions of someone who'd spent hundreds of hours on the slopes.

Raphael rolled the rest of the way over and onto his back. He began to laugh, looking up at the steely gray sky and the puffs of his steamy breath. He thought perhaps when his day was done and he returned to his cabin that he'd call up a certain video of Kammie and fantasize about what might've been.

4

"Hurry up," Renata Le Page said to the server hurrying into the kitchen via the back door.

Renata was Raphael's little sister—younger by eleven years—and he'd gotten her the job on the stipulation that she promised to follow all the rules and not put his standing in jeopardy with her poor decisions. Harsh, but fair. Her decisions had been the reason she was again unemployed, living with their parents, and seeing no future prospects. She'd agreed to everything he'd demanded and had managed to live up to all she'd promised. A big part of that was a change in location; sure, the drunken celebrities always trying for some last call action were tempting, but they didn't find the rubber in her arms like her friends back home. At Le Sommet, she had only circumstantial friends and her brother. Here, she'd even become a bit of a role model, whenever one of the younger women cared to see her that way.

"I know, I'm sorry," Jenna Cashman said, straightening her black skirt. She was trim with big breasts and a symmetrical face. Blonde. Beautiful. Short-sighted. "But you wouldn't believe it."

Renata gave her an eyebrow and a tilt of her hip. "Oh yeah," she said.

"Connor Murray and Leon Vogl were here last night and asked me to come to their chalet, so I went and we're going to party tonight," Jenna said, beaming.

Renata shook her head, visibly disappointed.

"What, it's not on the property? I can go—what?" Jenna said again when Renata continued shaking her head.

"Le Sommet owns the chalets too. They own everything but the roads and the mountains anywhere the slopes aren't."

Jenna pouted, but she'd already made up her mind. "Fine, I won't go, but think about it. What if I really hit it off with one of them, being a pro hockey player's wife is way more money than I'll ever earn waiting tables."

Renata figured a hockey player's wife would have to earn it in ways Jenna did not foresee, but didn't say that. "You make better money here than you would waiting tables anywhere outside maybe NYC or Paris or some wild Saudi Arabian place."

"I know," Jenna said. "But it's only for the winter."

Renata nodded toward the kitchen. This conversation had to stop; it was taking her back mentally to the party girl she'd been right before begging for this job. "In four months you earn, what, fifty-grand? That gives you eight months to do anything else."

"I know."

Through the rear doors of the kitchen, the smell of wine hit them like snowballs to the face. The chefs were creating a new dish and they both had glasses of red wine within reach and a pot of some kind of sauce on the go.

"Tell every customer who do not order de boeuf that they are fool," the younger chef said and grinned, his English hued heavily by French. His teeth were pink.

On the prep island were three young men massaging huge slabs of sirloin beef just waiting to be roasted. There were bowls of mixed spices and chopped onions as well. Imagining the end result made Renata's mouth water.

"You'd give up these kinds of perks to lay with some hockey players?" she whispered over her shoulder to Jenna.

Jenna sighed, "No, of course not."

They entered the dining room and got to the usual routine. One server was still on from the prior shift, but only two tables had patrons, and one of those tables was a nanny with two children, so they wouldn't even need drink refills.

5

Raphael finished with the rental skis that had come back that afternoon; waxed and leaned in their appropriate places on the wall. He'd worked in a good many ski shops before landing this job, but none where two of the four employees had been professionals; which was how the management came to call the ski shop a pro shop, like tennis or golf. The other pro was a snowboarder named Ross who spent a good portion of the day half-baked, but that fit. Snowboarders and marijuana were like centenarians and Velcro shoes.

A cool gust entered the shop as the bell on the door jangled. Raphael stood from where he'd crouched by rental boots and nodded to the trio of men stepping his way. He wondered if these were the scientists he was to babysit up the mountain, though they really did not look like scientists, more like TV tough guys.

"You Raphael Le Page?" Sidney asked

Raphael nodded. "You here to rent or…" He let it hang.

"We're here on official business. We booked you to take us up this mountain," Sidney said.

"Ah, right. Tomorrow morning, correct? I don't have my dates muddled?" Raphael said.

"Yeah, tomorrow, preferably after ten. I like my beauty sleep," Dusty said and Maurice elbowed him in the ribs. "What?"

"Okay. Uh, firstly, where exactly am I taking

you?" Raphael was now questioning the validity of what these men had said. Apparently, they were going up to take high-altitude samples in order to measure trade winds, but also collect a down weather balloon they'd lost sometime last year. It sounded legit in the email, but the edges had been frayed every extra moment he thought about it. Firstly, the email address had a Gmail tag instead of some dot gov or dot org. Next, the language surrounding the task was out of the ordinary, or rather, too ordinary. Scientists had come up before and most of them were exactly what you expected. And finally, none of the scientists from the contact sheet had any of their educational accolades listed after their names, which in Raphael's experience, when it came to the scientific and educational fields, doctors wore their accreditation and qualifications like Olympic medals.

"We got a GPS ping from the balloon and we figure we can look for a cave to get a sample. Got to be plenty of caves up there," Sidney said.

"Right. Can you give me the coordinates?" Raphael said. They hadn't in their email, as if it was some kind of secret.

"Sure thing," Dusty said and pulled out his cellphone. He'd taken the note as Sidney read it from his laptop before they flew all the way out here. "You ready?" He eyed Raphael.

"One second," he said and withdrew his Samsung S21, complete with satellite sleeve. He opened the app he used when taking special guests on extended cross-country treks. "Okay, go."

Dusty read it out and Raphael typed it in. He

then lifted his eyes and did a mental tally of what he thought each of these men might be capable of without too much trouble. It didn't add up to a strong result.

"And there's a fourth?" he said.

"Five. Got a research assistant coming along too. She's experienced, like us," Maurice said.

"This is at least three days up. Probably only one back if you know what you're doing," Raphael said.

"Didn't I just say we all got experience?" Maurice said.

Sidney touched his arm. "Why so long? Don't look too far to me."

"It's not, if we could go in a straight line, but we have to avoid a great mass of stone. Why aren't you going by helicopter?" Raphael said.

"We like fresh air," Sidney said—they weren't going by helicopter because they wanted as little trace coming back to them as possible. They'd given phony names, using mediocre phony IDs at check-in, and had paid with a burner credit card.

"How come we can't take snowmobiles?" Maurice said.

Raphael lifted an eyebrow—a gesture he and his sister had both learned from their mother. "You'd have to rent those in town and I say good luck if you didn't do that before you got here. Besides, snowmobiles wouldn't make it up how we'll have to go anyway. There'll be some small-scale climbing, which renders a snowmobile useless, even if you have one. Are you really certain you're up for this? You brought thermal camping gear, correct?"

They hadn't.

"Of course," Sidney said. "Look, we'll be fine. We maybe underestimated the distance some, but we can handle it."

Raphael began mulling over the options. He wasn't about to take these guys and their lab assistant up there to die, but Ross had a full schedule and the young guys who managed the rentals and cleanup would be busy; not that Raphael knew exactly what they could do, skill-wise. This was going to be a mess and Renata would be mad, but he'd have to rope her in.

"Look, you need to hire a second guide. Forgive my candidness, but you're out of your depth."

Dusty sneered and Maurice wore an expression like he wasn't used to this kind of back sass, but Sidney said, "Absolutely, that's a great idea." The other men looked at him with a mixture of surprise and confusion.

"All right then. I also don't think it wise that we wait until ten. Sunup will be at around a quarter after eight and I think we should be ready to go by then," Raphael said.

"Listen here, we hired—" Dusty started.

He was cut off by Sidney. "That sounds wise. As we've perhaps underestimated the trek, is there somewhere to purchase extra supplies?"

Raphael nodded. "Sure, head back down to Port Sur. Right on Main there's a very good shop."

"We were going to use a sled to bring down a fairly bulky and heavy sample, think that'll do?" Sidney said.

"Sure, but a sled built for the task, not like a

kids' sled," Raphael said, and normally he wouldn't be so blunt, but he foresaw a great big headache on the horizon and most of it would be thanks to the ineptitude of these men.

Sidney stayed quiet a few moments and then laughed. "See you tomorrow at eight, Ralphie."

"It's Raphael."

Sidney saluted and then turned. The others followed him out of the store, and once the door closed Sidney said, "That mouthpiece better win me over or he ain't making it down the mountain. We only need him going up, I figure."

6

The sports store was called, quite simply, SKI, though it had odds and ends in a range of many different winter sports. Two teenagers worked the floor—one helping a customer and the other stacking different types of waxes. A large, broad-shouldered man leaned against a display of ice skates and gave the group a grin.

"Let me guess, in for the week and doing some skiing?" he said. His voice was a booming baritone. This was Wesley Krup.

"Almost," Sidney said.

"Almost," the man parroted and then squinted. "Well, you have me stumped because you aren't local, and this time of year it's skiing."

"We're skiing," Sofia said, almost pouted it out as she eyed the muscular man.

"We're scientists and we're here to take samples from on high. Not all of our equipment arrived and some of the equipment that did, won't be, you know, enough," Sidney said.

The entire group had come because Sidney decided to not only take Raphael's advice, but to really play along. It came to him that the man might refuse to take them up the mountain if they seemed like it might cause him too much grief. Better to appear respectful and willing to listen.

"Ah, I get you. When do you head up the mountain?" Wesley said.

"First thing," Sidney said.

The others had begun milling around the store, touching things and checking price tags. Maurice whistled looking at the price of a set of DPS skis.

"So no ordering in from the city," Wesley said. "How about you tell me what you're up to and what you have. I'm guessing the mix-up with equipment is misunderstanding the terrain some?"

"You know, that's right on the nose. We misunderstood, happens to anybody," Sidney said and then explained the situation.

Sixty-nine minutes later, they all had new undergarments, better gloves, better headwear, aluminum snowshoes, two aluminum sleighs—used because that's all that was available—two new tents, a stack of campfire extras, and a little bit of knowhow they hadn't possessed when they'd entered. Sidney paid close to four-grand, using a mix of cash and pre-paid cards. If they didn't find that money, they'd have to pull a heist just to get home.

Sofia made a face looking at the bags of stuff. "You know, this is the first time I've gone shopping and didn't get a damned thing I wanted."

"You want to keep your ass from freezing, don't ya?" Riccardo said. He'd stood next to Wesley a few times, flexing his chest, as if comparing himself to the other man.

"Hopefully we don't meet again," Wesley said.

Sidney frowned. "Why's that? I thought we were getting along swimmingly."

Wesley gave a half-mouth grin. "I'm the private contractor Sommet use when they have a search and rescue issue that can be reached by snowmobile—

mostly broken legs or lost guests. Those sleds both trailed behind my snowmobile, at one time or another, hauling some poor sap down the mountain. I used to work for Sommet directly, but I didn't like the rules."

"The rules?" Sofia said.

"Lot of beautiful women stay there." Wesley made eyes at Sofia and then looked to Riccardo and winked. "It's hotel policy not to sleep with the guests."

Sidney laughed. "I like an entrepreneurial mind and a…a stiff resolve."

The rest laughed then and the two teenagers paused what they were doing to look at the group congregated by the door. Once the customers departed, Wesley said to a young woman Windexing the goggles display, "Ten bucks and my right arm says I'll be seeing those bozos again; probably I'll have to bring them down the mountain."

"You still owe me ten bucks and your right arm from last time you said that," the employee said.

"That wasn't my fault, turns out that lady hadn't made it off the kiddie hills," he said—the lady of note had purchased more than three-grand in high end ski equipment, spoke of being a quick learner and the eventual mastery of the sport. "No doubt those bozos will get *somewhere*."

7

Raphael plunked down at the mahogany bar and awaited his sister's notice. He'd already gone to his boss and then her boss to work out the logistics. She wouldn't be happy as it left her without much of a choice. Imagining her reaction had him cringing prematurely. In her youth, she'd had some doozies when it came to fits: one time she'd thrown a glass of water in their mother's face at a busy restaurant when she was informed that she wouldn't be going to a party, another time she'd taken their father's golf clubs to the flat screen after she found out the dentist had had an emergency and her braces would have to stay put until after the sophomore semi-formal. A bit of therapy and a bit more road separated that version of Renata and the current one, but Raphael couldn't help his memory or his imagination.

"Hey," Renata said from behind the bar. She was smiling wide and grabbing herself a glass of water from the fountain pop tap. "Drink?"

"No." Raphael inhaled a deep breath before laying it out in a brief sentence. "You have to come up the mountain with me tomorrow morning." The words almost jumbled with tension.

"What?" she said and put the glass to her mouth.

Raphael's eyebrows came together, as if physically pained. "I have to take rookies up the mountain and need help and you're the best suited. I already talked to both our bosses."

"So you're telling me, not asking?"

"Sort of."

Renata came around the bar and sat on the stool next to her brother. She set the glass down and put a hand on his shoulder. "You seem tense. Is it because this is wrong? Because you've put me in an awkward position?" Her fingers dug into the meat of his collar and he winced, curling himself away from the pain. "It's not just tomorrow, is it?"

Raphael spoke through the pain. "No, might be five days."

She let go suddenly. "Sounds fun." She let her hand fall and leaned shoulder to shoulder with him. "I wouldn't even have this job…I already have enough money in the bank to buy a used Honda. I've never had my own savings account."

Raphael sighed. "I'm proud of you. Well…I guess I'm mostly relieved." He leaned into her and their foreheads were almost touching.

"That's—" Renata started, but was interrupted.

The Kammie Kassion stood before them, her eyebrows lifted, but her forehead perfectly smooth thanks to a layer of collagen. "So I won't be seeing you," she said and pouted her lips. "Have a nice life, Raphael Le Page." And as quickly as she came, she left.

Renata watched her go as Raphael leaned back against the bar with his elbows, again looking pained, the hanging lights banking a yellow hue off his cheeks.

"You giving her lessons?" Renata hissed, amazed. It did not get much bigger than Kammie Kassion.

"Was."

"Oh?"

"She's leaving tomorrow. She's tried to fuck me all week."

Renata gasped. "No."

"Yes."

"Must be a rebound thing."

Raphael peeked at his sister with a squinted eye. "Thanks," he said.

"Might've been worth getting fired over," Renata said.

"I would've done it in a heartbeat ten years ago, but I think she mostly wanted me because I wasn't playing along…hardest thing I've had to do in quite a while."

"Ha, hardest," Renata said. "What time we heading out? You're packing the food and whatnot, right?"

Around them, the dinner crowd began to swell with an incoming group of twenty-somethings and Raphael could only nod and shout, "Meet here at seven. Forecast says it'll be cold."

8

A good sales day always put Wesley in the mood to take the snowmobile for a rip. While out, he decided he'd have a drink and see what kind of crop of women were at the bar. He'd spent his entire life having an easy time with the opposite sex. He wasn't exactly traditionally handsome, but he had a face that had obviously been punched and the kind of body that obviously punched back. He liked to think women saw him as dangerous.

The women were at the bar in abundance, but he hung back, nursing an American beer. In the VIP section, among others, he saw a disinterested looking Kammie Kassion. She was blowing off potential suiters as if they were flies and a notion formed: *she's bored.* Eventually she stood, asked a server for her parka and started toward the private balcony.

Wesley paid his tab in haste and hurried out to where he'd parked the snowmobile. He buzzed around to the back of the hotel and then skirted a barricade that kept average patrons and paparazzi away. The pitch upward had the machine barking, but he got around the barricade and then zoomed toward the balcony. He stopped below.

Kammie was looking down at him from about ten feet above. He pulled off his helmet and rose from the seat.

"You're bored," he said.

"How could I be?" she said.

"Easy, and I can tell."

"Oh yeah."

"I can show you something you've never seen before."

Kammie snickered. "Sure you can."

"Take us half an hour on the sled, going just about straight up the mountain."

"What is it?" she said.

"Glacial cave. Some of that ice is more than one hundred thousand years old."

"Really? Why isn't that on the brochure?"

Wesley could tell he almost had her sold. "Two reasons. One: it's protected by the government. Two: it's too dangerous for unskilled visits."

"And just how skilled are you supposed to be?" she said.

Wesley pointed at the word stenciled on his snowmobile's hood: RESCUE. "I'm the bar they measure skill against…and I'm pretty good at the rescue stuff, too. You coming?"

She pondered it just a few seconds. "I guess. I'll come around—"

"Jump," he said, not wanting to allow her any time for separation and chances at second thoughts.

"What?"

"Jump. I'll catch you."

"You must be kidding," she said, leaning over the balcony to gauge the distance.

"I'll catch you."

"You're crazy."

"Think you'll get a chance to play Romeo and Juliet over a balcony again?" Wesley said and that did it. This was new and different and she was indeed very bored.

"If you miss me…"

Wesley knew what would happen, but she was like a sprite, a buxom sprite. "I wouldn't let you fall."

Kammie pulled out her phone. She sent a text that explained where she was going and then snapped a shot of Wesley, texted it along too. She hadn't brought along security, but security always kept tabs, which was good and bad. She pocketed the phone and then climbed over the railing. She turned and faced Wesley again. He'd repositioned himself with his arms out to cradle her landing.

"You ready?" she said.

"Whenever you are," he said.

She closed her eyes and then stepped off. It was only a second before she landed against the sturdy arms. She wrapped her arms around his neck, heart racing, excitement flaring wonderfully.

"You caught me," she said, purred it even.

"We're only just beginning. I'll do much more than catch you," he said and lowered her so her feet were on the ground. He handed her the helmet from the bench seat. "Keep that face perfect."

"Thanks," she said and pulled on the helmet.

Wesley grabbed goggles from the storage hold and zipped the collar of his coat up to the bottom of his ears. "Get behind me and hang on. Tight."

He sat and then she sat with her thighs pressed snugly against him. Her hands were inside her sleeves, arms wrapped around his hard middle. Wesley basked a moment in the heat coming from the peak between her legs.

He then thumbed the ignition and they were off up the hill.

9

The lounge where the guys went was secluded enough that they could converse without yelling, but the hip-hop music from the dancefloor still hit them loud and clear. Sidney suggested they all hit the sack after their second, post-supper drink.

"I'm going to see if these nachos are any good," Dusty said. Like the others, he'd already downed a huge serving of beef roast with mashed potatoes, a dinner roll, and then chocolate mousse for dessert.

"Think we'll kick around for another drink," Riccardo said.

Sofia was up and half dancing about ten feet away, secretly ripping off farts.

"A wise man gets a good rest before a big day, big week even," Sidney said, but said nothing more. He and Maurice headed to the elevators and were quickly gone from sight and mind.

"Tequila?" Riccardo said.

Sofia hooted. They ordered three rounds to start and Dusty demolished a plate of nachos. By ten o'clock, they were drunk and on the dance floor. The crowd was mostly youthful, but a sprinkling of middle-aged men of wealth added some salt to the pepper.

Dusty polished off a few more beers before heading off to his room. Riccardo had begun to slow by midnight and sat at a table not far from where Sofia danced. She spied him from where she was and then slowly backed into a trio of young men and women. One man targeted Sofia and immediately began grinding against her. She bit her lip and popped her ass into the man's crotch to a Pharrell beat.

Riccardo watched for two songs, knowing what Sofia was up to. The guy got handsy and started sucking Sofia's neck like a geriatric vampire who has misplaced their dentures. That did it and Riccardo walked across the floor with his beer glass in hand. Without a word, he slammed the glass over the young man's head, spraying beer all over.

"You lug!" Sofia shouted, wet.

Three guys tried to circle in on Riccardo but he whipped out a butterfly knife, dancing it into deadly shape. "Come on, who's first?" he said.

The trio lifted their hands and backed away. Sofia was already stomping toward the washrooms when a big man in a black suit tapped on Riccardo's shoulder. Riccardo turned and the security guard nailed him in the jaw, crumpling him. The crowd cheered and Riccardo slammed up a foot into the big—though no bigger than Riccardo—man's testicles. He crumpled. As Riccardo began to rise, two friends of the buddy with a head wound jumped on him. The knife slashed once and then a second time.

Riccardo stood and discreetly pocketed his knife as two more men in black suits headed his way. Bloody and exhilarated, Riccardo bolted into the busy crowd and out onto a verandah only five feet above a snowbank.

While Riccardo was on the move, Sofia was in the washroom. She dabbed at her dress, pissed because it was the only night she'd get to wear it while they were there. A toilet paper roll thumped as it spun and then a flush followed. A young woman in tights and a too large sweater stepped out of a stall licking her gums and wiggling her nose.

"Hey," Sofia said, looking at the woman via reflection. A fantastic idea struck.

The woman looked back using the same mirror. "Hey, yourself."

"I have a long few days ahead of me, know where I can get some pick me up?"

"I don't know what you mean." The woman moved her jaw around as she spoke.

Sofia rolled her eyes. "Bitch, there's coke under your nose."

The woman stiffened and inspected her reddened nostrils. "No there's not."

"Maybe not, but there'll be more there later. Come on, show me some love."

The woman worked her jaw more and *Bewitched* twitched her nose. "Fine. I'll text my guy."

Sofia watched and waited. She'd silently worried how in the hell she was going to make it days skiing and snowshoeing, mostly uphill. The woman slipped her phone back into the Coach clutch she carried.

"He'll come to the hallway in ten minutes. If you're not there, he'll leave." The woman walked by Sofia and out of the toilet.

An attendant stood by the door, staring straight ahead. "If the guy's named Greg, come back in and I'll make a call," the attendant said.

Sofia considered this. "Greg no good?"

"Greg cuts everything with baby powder and baking soda. Fine for rookies," the attendant said, still looking at the wall across the room.

"If you call your friend, how do I get what I want?"

"What do you want?"

"Speed, or coke if there's no speed."

A trio of drunk young women stumbled into the washroom, loud and raucous. Sofia took a ten out of her purse and put it in the attendant's cup, taking a breath mint.

"Do you smoke?" the attendant said, smiling and nodding at Sofia.

"Cigarettes? Sometimes."

The attendant pulled a pack of Marlboros from her pocket and shook one free. Sofia accepted it. "Only place you can smoke and not freeze to death is in the parking garage," the attendant said.

Sofia got it and headed out. The parking garage was accessible via the elevators by the main lobby. It took a few minutes to cross the hotel, but an open elevator awaited her. She rode it down. Once there, she stepped away from the elevator and fished a lighter from her purse. She lit and waited.

As the cigarette reached the filter, a Jeep Cherokee pulled up and a window rolled down. The man inside said, "My friend said you might get cold smoking down here."

Sofia dropped the cigarette, opened the door, and fell in. She was cold. The man began driving. He wore a knit sweater and two gold rings. He smelled pleasantly manly; she wished Riccardo would switch off the cheap shit cologne.

"Hey," she said.

"You need uppers?"

"Speed," she said.

"I have this stuff called Kenzedrine; no powder or crystal. And coke, of course."

"Kenzedrine? That pharma or home brew?" she said, not that she was much of an expert, more like she was asking the price.

"Pharma," the man said, looking offended. "Always pharma and I don't cut anything. Kenzedrine is my personal go to. You're invincible for three to six hours; for me, it's always four hours and forty minutes, clockwork. So dependable and you feel like someone filled your veins with nitrous."

Sofia nodded as she opened her purse. Riccardo had promised they'd have millions by next week, maybe more than one hundred million if the rest of the crew died in the plane crash, so she'd upped her credit card limit over the telephone and then withdrew ten thousand in cash. She'd get what she needed, and thought she might get enough for everyone else, then demand a whole chunk of the cash afterward. Make her an official partner.

"I need a quarter of coke and I don't know, fifteen…Kenzedrines?"

The man's eyebrows shot up and he took a hard turn in the opposite direction he'd been driving. "I certainly don't have that on me. Show me the cash—I don't do that blowjob's worth a mint stuff."

Sofia might've been offended under other circumstances, but instead, she pulled out her wallet and a thick stack of one hundred Euro bills. "And here, I scored a mint, just in case," she said and took the white candy she'd gotten from the bathroom attendant and popped it in her mouth.

"I call them Kennies, like Bennies," the dealer said.

Within minutes, he parked and invited Sofia inside.

"How about we make this quick?"

The man said nothing and popped out of the Jeep to run inside. Within ten minutes, she was back at the resort and riding the elevator up. Riccardo was awake and pissed when she got back to the room, but he cooled when she wasn't any drunker than before and she promised to give him a surprise tomorrow.

He was sullen as they watched a Japanese gameshow, but he started snoring before 2:00 AM. Sofia shut down the TV shortly after and started counting minks and purses and shoes, all the fabulous crap she'd buy when she was rich.

10

Kammie Kassion wasn't the only woman Wesley had taken to the glacier cave, and after that first visit—with a woman named Lacy, or maybe Stacy—he'd gone up during the day to stash some things. The room flickered, the orange and yellow flames dancing from the portable fire pit he'd set atop a square of aluminum. Kammie and Wesley sat on a water-resistant sleeping bag with a padded bottom.

"You're right, I've never seen anything like this," Kammie said, finally. She'd been a bit sullen when they first arrived. The trip had taken every second of the promised thirty minutes, and it had been cold. Extremely cold. But now that she was warming up and understood the singular beauty around her, she could appreciate the effort it took to get there. "That blue reminds me of snow cones after you've sucked away most of the syrup."

Wesley snickered. "You don't seem like the snow cone type of girl."

"I'm not, not anymore. Kids eat them and I ate them as a kid."

"But you're not a kid anymore." Wesley leaned close and nudged her. "Tell me more about you as a kid."

A thought came to Kammie and she opened her mouth, but decided against telling the stranger about the fabulous dolls her mother and father had bought her, ones that she couldn't touch in case her childish dexterity ruined them, and how she had a stash of Barbies and Cabbage Patch Kids she'd collected from the attic from when she was little-little. Instead, thinking about needing to sleep and the long trek home, she said, "No." She unzipped her parka and lay back. She unbuttoned her pants to reveal stretchy, black, crotchless thermals. Beneath were lacy beige panties. Steam rose from the indented crevice at the center. "Come on, I've had a fruitless week."

Wesley worked fast, taking off his bulky coat and then boots. His snow pants slipped down over his jeans. His eyes were hard on Kammie. She'd lifted her sculpted ass and slid her pants down and unzipped one boot to free a leg. The thermals went to her ankles in a tight roll and Wesley paused to see just how much nudity Kammie cared to reveal.

Kammie pushed up then and opened Wesley's fly, doing her best to hold eye contact—his snow pants were only down to his thighs. She reached in and found an engorged cock that was not easily maneuvered through the fly of his boxer shorts, but did find its way out.

"God," Wesley groaned.

Her mouth was blazing on the frosty air. Her hand pushed aside the slim track of her panties and her fingers played it the uppermost reaches of the cleft. Wesley put a hand on her head and led her on his rhythm. She played along, but allowing him to drive only so deeply. At the first twinge of peaking, he reached into his pocket, past his wallet, past his cellphone, and to the rubber he'd put there before heading up to Le Sommet.

"Your turn," he said.

Kammie gave a final long slurp at the head of his cock and then backed off in order to stretch out. She brought her knees up—pants bunched around her left calf—and spread her thighs. Wesley was already down and crawling toward that fantastically hot space. He sidelined her panties again and used two fingers to spread her lips. Her pussy tasted metallic and a bit soapy. It smelled perfect, her musk light and appealing. He traced along with the tip of his tongue until he found that pocket protecting her clit. He dug in and drew circles with his tongue while his free hand slipped into the deep, wet gorge.

She whined gently, encouraging Wesley to continue. He did and with renewed vigor, though he pulled his hands away to fiddle with the condom. The gold wrapper fell and the rubber slipped on like a second skin. His mouth came away from her sex and he leaned over her. Their mouths came together and she tasted herself and he tasted himself. Her right hand guided him inside and he began thrusting, driving into her with a steady and heavy motion. Steam clouded around them like fog. A breathy pant like a smoker's cough began at the back of Wesley's throat and Kammie moaned with regular hitching breaths; neither heard the swishing footfalls or the low growl as something raced into the cave.

"Keep go-oh-oh-ohing." Kammie opened her eyes and tilted her head back.

Above them was a beast. It had to be eight feet tall. Thick white fur covered its immense body and the flesh of its face was pale blue. Slobber ran down from its jaws in sticky tendrils.

Kammie screamed and Wesley gave a final pulsating thrust into her, assuming that scream was for him. She attempted to push him off, but he had to be twice her weight.

"There's a gorilla!" she screamed in Wesley's ear.

Now he did turn over. That was no gorilla. "No fuck!" he shouted and the huge paws with fat, fat fingers reached for him.

Kammie rolled away, sending the gas fire pit onto its side. The beast was on Wesley, his legs kicking and his hands digging for purchase into the furry back. It held Wesley's right arm and punched at his chest. The arm tore free and a geyser of steamy liquid fountained out. Bloody bubbles gurgled from his lips and the beast went in for a bite.

Kammie saw her chance and grabbed her boot. With one bare foot and her pants around her thigh, she hopped onto the snowmobile, sending the helmet to the icy floor where it spun like a top. She watched over her shoulder as she reefed the leather boot on—the beast was eating, smacking its blood-red maw.

She gasped and tried to shake away the image, focusing instead on the dash of the snowmobile. Everyone treated her like a princess, like a doll, but she'd done it all and while she wasn't overly intelligent, she understood how things worked once she'd used them. She pressed her thumb against the start button and the snowmobile rumbled to life. She thumbed down hard on the accelerator. The track spun and on the second revolution caught against the ice, jerking the sled violently enough that she nearly slipped off the back.

A little slower, but much too fast for comfort, she navigated between the walls of the deep glacier cave. Nine times a ski struck a protruding lip that rose next to another ice wall, but she finally saw the unreflective wall of night before her. She thumped the throttle hard and burst out into the night.

At the mouth of the cave, a furry white arm came down on her and clawed fingers dug into her eye sockets. The snowmobile rocketed down the mountain, rolling until it came to a stop behind a thick copse of fir trees.

Kammie Kassion's final thought was, *how'd you get out so fast—oh! Two!* before the even larger beast bent down and took her perfectly sculpted face into its hands and began peeling for its favorite bit of meat.

11

Raphael awoke briefly from a dream that had jarred him, though he didn't recall what it was. He blinked at the clock. It was after 2:00 AM. Out the window of his homey little cabin, snow drifted lazily down from higher up on the mountain, breaking up the solidity of the black night.

His last night in the cozy warmth for five or six days—a depressing thought.

He rolled over and closed his eyes. He needed to sleep, but something nagged him about the group. Still, he refused himself the luxury of getting up and finding a distraction. He checked the clock nine more times before he eventually fell back asleep.

12

Jenna hurried through the process of straightening up after last call. She'd already done her till and tipped the kitchen staff a small chunk from her night on the floor—a custom that she begrudgingly understood. She had to get out to the chalet before long or the guys would be asleep and she'd be risking her job for nothing. She preferred Connor, but would drive a barbed hook into either if it meant luxury coming her way as opposed to purveyed by her in the workplace.

In high school she'd dated football players and understood how athletes were; young ones anyway. These guys were in their late twenties, but she suspected they weren't so different from the boys in high school.

Outside in her bulky coat—a gift from her father that turned out to be more than a size too big, but was cozy enough to ignore the ill fit—she began texting as she walked: *on my way.*

Connor responded: *we almost gave up on you.* He then added a smiley face followed by a peach and then an eggplant.

Oh she'd get that barbed hook into him yet. She began imagining some grand game plan where she teased him along, but it wouldn't work from a straight angle. Hockey players could get gorgeous women in their beds whenever they wanted; she had to dangle something better. She began running. She had two excellent sets of Victoria Secret that played to her curves like nothing else.

Soon: she texted back, keeping her speed up as she broke between cars in the uncovered lot and through the tunnel that led down to the apartments on the edge of the property. They were tiny, more like dorm rooms than apartments—aside from that she needn't share a bathroom or kitchen.

Inside, she dropped her purse and stripped. She showered, careful to keep her hair dry, and then spritzed scent anywhere that might smell like food or that might reveal that she was a living human being with bodily functions. She slipped into a pink and black lace and silk chemise. She rolled the inch of skirt up and stepped into black yoga pants. She put on a bulky sweater with a collar loose enough that if she leaned the right ways, it would reveal what she had on beneath.

Back into her boots and jacket, she ran for her ten-year-old Fiat and buzzed up the mountain to the chalets. She passed Beamers and Benzes, a Maybach, a Bentley, and then reached the spot with the lifted F-250 truck. She slipped in next to the vehicle and Leon came running in just boxer shorts and a fur hat. Snow speckled his body. A young woman chased him, perhaps a local, laughing as she fired a water gun.

Jenna frowned, but kept on and entered the chalet. It was empty, but on the rear deck was a hot tub. Two more young women sat in the bubbling water with two frumpy guys she'd never seen before. She huffed; this was not the kind of party she had in mind. She put a hand on her purse, thinking she'd text Connor and—

"Hey," Connor said, stepping from the kitchen with a bottle of beer in hand.

"Hi," Jenna said back, suddenly feeling much better. "How come you're not out there partying it up?"

Connor looked through the wall of windows. "I would be; last night was my last night for booze. We've got a game in three days. Can't drink like I used to…and I'm only up on Matthews by two points for the league lead."

"Oh," she said. She'd crossed the distance and stood before him. "Leon's drinking."

"He's German," Connor said, as if that answered it.

Jenna tittered and put a hand on Connor's muscular forearm.

"You don't mind, do you? I thought maybe you and me could hang out, alone."

Jenna nibbled the inside of her bottom lip a moment and then said, "No, I was hoping you'd say that."

13

The snow continued a sparse and lazy fall. The temperature had warmed greatly from the day previous, leaving everything crunchy and slick, but agreeable. Raphael had begun explaining the route, his sense of calm rescued by the professional equipment and clothing these so-called scientists had with them. He took in the faces: a few looking overwrought, but possibly they just had that *I slept in a hotel and got up too early, what do you expect* expression.

"Do you care, or do you just want to follow me?" he said.

"Lead us, oh wise one," Sidney said.

"Okay. First bit is almost straight up, so snowshoes instead of skis." Raphael lifted his well-worn pair in case any of them forgot which was which. He bent to slip his feet in, his heavy pack making it much easier to reach down than it would be to straighten up. "Everyone, this is my sister, Renata, she'll be bringing up the rear and making sure none of you stray."

Renata gave a flimsy wave.

"Two outdoors-folk in one family," Sidney said and tipped an imaginary cap.

"Can we just go already," Sofia said. She was saving the first trip down the fast lane for when Sidney or Maurice started looking tired—they were the ones to impress.

"I suppose we ought to," Raphael said. They'd

already gone through his checklist and then some. "Follow me. Let me know if I'm going too fast."

Around them, the first skiers and snowboarders of the day milled the flat beneath one of the hills, not quite heading for the ski-lift. Unfortunately, the ski-lift and regularly used hills were on the far side of a jutting rock formation or taking the lift would've saved the trek up the mountain some time and energy.

The sun peeked over the white caps and kept coming just as they took their first steps. Raphael watched over his shoulder and immediately had to slow his already plodding pace. He thought, *they get better as they get practiced* and *why in the hell haven't they already practiced?* The big guys— Dusty and Riccardo—pulled the sleighs with most of the gear. Both had sweat running down their faces despite the intense chill.

At the fifty-one minute mark, Sidney shouted, "Break time!"

Raphael looked back and realized he'd gotten in the zone. The closest, Maurice, was twenty-five yards behind him. Raphael let his body tip and timbered down into the snow. They'd never even come close at this rate, great weather and nice hard snow were wasted on these people.

Renata stepped around the group of wheezing men and one woman, and hurried up to her brother. "This is going to take forever. That woman's fallen sixteen times now and I think Dusty shit his pants."

"They've paid, so I guess we go until they beg us to stop." Raphael looked up at his sister then, her features hidden in shadow. "How you doing?"

"Been a while since I've been on snowshoes, but it's easier than waiting tables and nobody's trying to grab my ass."

"Happen a lot?"

Renata huffed. "Enough." She exhaled a deep breath that departed like she'd dragged off a vape stick. "What do you think, we even make it to the glacier caves today?"

Raphael whistled. "We should make it there in a couple of hours. Should've maybe paid Wes to lug them up that far."

The glacial caves were just about the furthest a snowmobile could go and get to where they were headed.

"There's something funny, right? It's not just me?" Renata said.

"What?"

"With them."

Raphael pulled his right hand from his glove to watch the steam rise. "If they're scientists, I'm an astronaut. Seem more like hoods."

"So why in the hell are they wanting to go up the mountain?" Renata said.

"Beats me. Help me up." Raphael held out his hands and Renata pulled. "All right, we need to move."

There were groans, but nobody argued. Renata stepped back from the path she and Raphael had stomped and let the others shamble by her. Things continued as they had before for about twenty minutes, then Sofia picked up her pace drastically and began shouting at the others to move. Sidney and Maurice sped up a few minutes later. Riccardo stopped lagging, despite dragging a sleigh. Then even Dusty had energy.

Renata didn't know what to make of it, but found she had to put real effort in to keep pace. By hour four, they'd passed one of three known openings of the glacial caves. Raphael had offered to stop so they could get samples, but Sidney and Sofia both shouted, "No!" and the trek continued.

Then Sofia began to slow some. The others did as well. The pace was good, covering area, and making decent time. Raphael had to call the next stop and everyone paused on his command.

It seemed impossible that these people were suddenly so useful and agreeable, but they were, and when Renata fell into the snow next to her brother, Raphael said, "What's your guess, caffeine pills or something stronger?"

"Ah, I hadn't even thought of that. I felt like we were on a prank show or something," Renata said as she uncapped a thermos of coffee. Steam billowed even under a fine sunray.

Distantly, dual snowmobile engines roared. Renata looked at Raphael with eyebrows raised. A few local companies had rental snowmobiles in town, but nobody was to go on the hotel side of the mountain, especially when it was busy like it was now.

"Some rich assholes likely," Raphael said.

He dug into his pack and found the stash of energy bars. He offered one to Renata. She accepted. Sidney stepped to them, munching on a high-sodium meat stick still halfway sheathed.

"This is a short break, yeah? We'll want a good

sleep, so given the time, we should probably move along soon, yeah?" Sidney said; he was wide-eyed and speaking quickly.

"Sure thing," Raphael said.

Sidney offered up something like a smile and hurried back to the group. They huddled up and then almost simultaneously slugged from water bottles and then jerked their heads back.

"They're taking something," Renata said.

"Whatever keeps them moving," Raphael said and re-donned his gloves. He pushed to his feet and addressed the others. "After another half-hour or so, we'll have to cut around a rock face, which means skis. It's the first major deviation from a straight line, but it can't be helped. At the edge of the rock face, it'll likely be close enough to sundown to break out the tents—if we keep the same pace and you all figure out skis as quickly as you did snowshoes."

"Let's move then!" Sofia said and trudged forward.

Renata shrugged at Raphael and he shouldered his pack. He stepped out just in front of Sofia and kept the parade moving. He imagined they looked like ants scaling a salt pile. Once the others passed her, Renata fell in and trailed the group. As it had before, it lagged and then new energy crept in—all but Sofia, her energy was steadily higher than that of the others.

It wasn't long before a piece of Renata wished she had some of whatever the others had, but shook off the thought. That wasn't even the old her, that was simply a semi-exhausted her. She hadn't fully comprehended how tiring this trip was going to be, but she was starting to get it.

The shadows were growing longer and the left foot right foot steadiness lulled her away until the group stopped and she nearly tripped over Dusty's sleigh. Clumsily, everyone took off their snowshoes. Renata leaned against the dark stone outcropping that rose as if punched from the Earth. There was a thick ledge at about eye-level and she paused. The snow had crusted and gone to ice, but it looked like half of an immense footprint, a single toe, long and visible, hung at the end like the dot to an exclamation point. The ice at the rear moon of the indentation was reddish pink, a color similar to cream soda syrup. A long white hair was trapped in the ice. She reached out her mitten, but didn't quite touch it. She decided the effort was beginning to weigh heavily on her and that hair was probably the kind of thing blown in from another continent, the very thing a scientist might find interesting. She considered calling out to Sidney, but decided against it when it became obvious that she'd be the last body with skis on her feet.

"Everybody ready, or do we need a break?" Raphael said, his nose was damp and his cheeks were rosy, but he looked lively.

"Move!" Sofia said, visibly stoned. She stamped her skis to show just how much she wanted to boogie.

14

Leon was slow to rise and Connor spent the early morning hours showing Jenna how to drive a snowmobile. Throughout, Jenna regularly checked her phone for the time. She had a work shift she wasn't exactly sure she was going to attend. The boys were leaving sooner than later, and the tighter she got, the more likely it'd be that Connor brought her along when he left. She hoped.

Aside from having sex twice, they'd talked for hours. She listened mostly as Connor had a great deal to tell about himself. She guessed that was what it would be like if there was a long run, almost as if dating a grown teenager, of course they weren't really dating…not yet.

"What time's your shift?" Connor said. He sat on the back of the snowmobile, his arms wrapped around Jenna, hands inside her jacket, rubbing fingertips against the silkiness of her chemise.

The engine ticked with melting water, but was silent otherwise. Jenna leaned back harder against Connor, his hands dipped below the waistband of her yoga pants, as she pulled her cellphone from the little zippered pocket.

"I work at noon, but—" She paused abruptly; while checking the time she read the alerts: one for a missed call and the other for a voicemail. The call was from work and assumedly the voicemail was as well. "They called me," she said then and dialed her mailbox.

She hit the speaker button and Connor's fingers brushed against the soft, waxed skin above her vagina. His pinky dipped like a fountain pen into an ink well.

"Jenna," her boss' voice said, "you know the rules. You cannot visit guests in their rooms, chalets, or cottages. You're fired, effective immediately."

Her chest hitched. This was very, very bad. If Connor had no future plans for her then—

"Guess you're free to come hang out, watch me play some hockey," he said and his hands trailed deeper, pushing open her thighs. "Would you like that?"

"Yes," she whispered, eyes closed.

"Do you like this?" he said, rubbing faster in a tight circle with one hand while clutching her thigh with the other.

"Yes," she whispered again.

"I want to fuck you," he said and trailed his sticky hands over the chemise.

She stood, leaning against the handlebars. She looked back and saw that he'd opened his pants. She scanned the vast whiteness around the chalet, making sure nobody was watching, and then lowered her pants before sitting down against him. He grabbed her around the waist and lifted for precision, thrusting into her as he did so.

The motion continued, mostly without rhythm. Wet flesh slapped and smacked. Connor's breath became heavier and Jenna squeezed the walls tight against his manhood. The hot splash inside her pulsed and triggered her own orgasm—the biggest part of this being that she didn't need to think about the future right away—though didn't quite follow through. He gave a handful of final, minute pushes and she slumped against him, seeking out his mouth with her mouth.

"We still going skating in that glacier the sport store guy told us about?" Leon asked.

Jenna and Connor whipped their heads around. Leon was in his boxer shorts, the fur hat, and untied boots. He was eating a banana.

"How long—?" Jenna started.

Connor cut her off, laughing as he said, "Get the hell out of here!"

Leon looked at Jenna and then back to Connor. "Okay," he said and turned, but stopped after one step. "Oh yeah, you told me to remind you to drink some Pepto Bismol because the food's been giving you diarrhea."

"Fuck off," Connor said, still laughing.

"Oh, and three old girlfriends called to inform you that they'd passed on STDs. Sorry. Oh, and your mom's pregnant; you really shouldn't have done that, it's just plain wrong," Leon said as he started away.

Connor tapped at Jenna's sides and pushed her up. He slid off the snowmobile bench seat—his flaccid penis slipping back into his pants like a turtle head—and leapt onto Leon's back. Leon screeched at the cold and Jenna saw her future, babysitting hunky adults; it had to be better than serving tables.

"You are both nuts," she said and stood, did a waddle all the way back into the chalet to find the toilet.

When she came out of the washroom, she gave a quick nod to the two frumpy men in the kitchen. The young women from the night before had disappeared and Jenna felt like she'd won some unnamed competition. Connor hurried in through the door overlooking the deck. He was soaked.

"Do you have skates?" he asked as he stepped by.

"No," Jenna said.

"Can you skate?"

"No."

He stopped for a moment, shrugged, and then continued on. "Guess you'll just have to watch us."

Leon came in next. His boxers were ripped and his hat looked like a swamp rat. "Can you skate?" he said.

"No."

"Oh," he said and then said something in German to the big guys. He focused on Jenna again. "They're like you, can't skate either."

"Come on, man!" Connor shouted as he emerged from his room with a new outfit on.

Leon ran by, the hole in his boxers giving a free show. When he was gone from eyeshot, Connor leaned close to Jenna.

"You know he was lying. I don't have any diseases."

"Okay," she said. "Neither do I."

"I sure hope not."

Things were a bit chaotic around her for the next ten minutes. Leon and Connor buzzed like hummingbirds, gathering what they'd need for an afternoon skating on one-hundred-thousand-year-old ice.

"Actually, you can shoot for the 'gram. It's perfect that you don't skate," Connor said.

"Ugh, phone!" Leon said and ran to his room.

Fifteen minutes later, Jenna was on the back of Connor's rented snowmobile while he buzzed along behind Leon. Paranoid about losing her purse, she'd draped the strap over her chest and then forced it inside and to the back of her coat. They cut up the path and raced by skiers going in the opposite direction. Wesley from the sports store had promised them the perfect spot to have a once in a lifetime skate in exchange for some saleable signatures on things; he'd also told them where to rent snowmobiles.

The sun was nice, but the wind had bite. Jenna buried her uncovered face in Connor's shoulder—he hadn't offered her the helmet he wore. This didn't bother her more than the nip of the chill. She closed her watery eyes and imagined their wedding. He was just about the biggest thing going when it came to hockey, the next Gretzky many informed hockey heads had said, so when it came to their nuptials, the celebration would have to be massive. She'd go to one of those outrageous stores in New York City or Paris or Montreal or Zurich. Her gown would need real live cherubs floating along behind her because the train would continue for yards. And the ring!

Connor slowed and the engine's growl dissipated. She opened her eyes to the incredible change in light and temperature. It was evening-dim and had to be ten degrees cooler. Up front, Leon clicked on his snowmobile's headlights. Connor did the same after a moment of searching the handlebars. The light banking back at them was incredible. They passed the first chamber and Leon flared his engine and spun the back end of his sled around in a sloppy one-eighty. None noticed the scores in the ice surface near the wall where Kammie Kassion had barely made a corner during her doomed escape attempt.

The engines died, but the lights remained lit, banking and meeting up with the shaft of outdoor light that made it as far as the second chamber. All the edges and their reflections made it feel like being inside a dirty blue gem stone. If someone buffed the place, it would probably shine. Though, perfection in nature usually felt phony.

Connor rose from the seat and took two steps and then slid five feet. He repeated this twice more to get to Leon who had the big backpack with the skates and the pucks. The two sticks they'd brought were strapped to the runners of Leon's sled and a chunky coat of snow clung to the blades.

Jenna turned on her seat and watched the men do what they did, and after a short warm-up, both skated to her with their phones.

"Take a bunch of shots with both," Connor said after he unlocked his iPhone.

Leon held his iPhone before his face and unlocked it. "Shout if it locks up," he said.

"Mine too!" Connor shouted from across the cavern. He was lightning on skates.

They carved into the ice, the grinding sound

echoing loudly off the walls and ceiling. Leon whistled and Jenna scooped up his phone—she'd taken two shots with Connor's and was simply pawing at Leon's screen to keep it from locking. He wound back for a slap shot and she took two quick shots before thumbing it to video. She caught his follow through and continued recording him. The puck nailed a stalagmite of ice and then the rounded base of the wall, causing it to loop-de-loop and then disappear into the next cavern. She lowered his phone when he chased after the puck, into the darkness.

"Nice shooting, soon they'll be comparing that laser to Ryan Smyth!" Connor shouted and skated closer to Jenna.

"Who's Ryan Smyth?" she said.

Connor pulled to a stop, sending a moderate snow shower washing from his blades. "Captain Canada," he said, as if that answered it. "Worst shot a great player ever had. He—"

An incredible growl echoed out from the chamber next-door. And then Leon screamed. Connor was off in a flash and Jenna could only sit and watch the opening to the next chamber. She heard another growl, and then a second that played atop the first. Connor made a noise she didn't like, so started the engine of the sled, thinking maybe they'd fallen into a chasm and the glacial acoustics had skewed their screams. She thumbed the gas and the sled jerked forward. She did it again and got the same result. She was twenty feet from the mouth of the third chamber when something huge and white charged out on its fours.

"Holy," she said, barking it out like a cough.

She thumbed the throttle and yanked the handlebars away from the depths. The cold bit at her and she instinctively got very low on the sled, squinting as she approached the light of the world. The beasts growled behind her, but she didn't dare look back.

"Polar b—"

A long white arm swung at her and she ducked so low her chin hit the top of the handlebars. Her teeth snapped together and granules from a newly busted filling coated the back of her tongue like chewed Tylenol. The arm had missed and she bolted straight forward, not thinking about getting down and getting help, not really thinking at all. She didn't look back until she'd made good space between her and the beasts. It was as if they were part of the snow; she only saw them because she knew they were there and were taking long strides on their hind legs.

Not bears, she thought and turned to face the direction she headed. Her left ski struck a huge outcropping rock face and she flew over the handlebars. She thumped heavily into the crunchy snow and her hand immediately went to the cut above her left eye. *Get up! They're coming!* a voice in her head shouted and she popped to her feet, cold and wet, but beating the count.

A piece of luck helped her; heading straight ahead was a smoothened and packed trail. She could run on a terrain like that; uphill was rock and downhill was deep snow that would be impossible to run through, unless she found another trail. The beasts had slowed enough that she didn't see them every time she looked, but understood they were just biding their time. Likely, this was how they hunted; wear out the prey and pick a meal when it became convenient. Tears sprang to Jenna's eyes and began freezing on her cheeks.

Ahead, distantly, she saw salvation. People, the same people who tamped this path for her. Maybe they'd have guns or knives. If she could get close enough, she'd start screaming, but until then, she prayed one would turn around.

15

Skiing proved easier to all but Dusty. He fell regularly, swearing and punching the snow around him. This left Dusty and Renata falling behind some. She'd tried to help him a few times, but he shrugged her off until finally on the sixth fall in an hour, he couldn't get up and angrily unclipped the harness for the sleigh of equipment he dragged.

Renata was no Olympian, but compared to average, she was pretty close to a master. As Dusty kicked and rolled, losing both skis in the process, Renata strode by him and reached down for the harness. Ahead, nobody had noticed that they'd stopped, so if something happened between then and the end of the day, there could be trouble.

If they didn't catch up.

The cross strap clicked with a thick plastic buckle and Renata grabbed the tails of both shoulder straps and yanked until the harness was tight. Dusty was on his knees, red-faced, sweaty, and scowling. His pupils were so big that his irises had almost disappeared, despite it being very bright out there.

"Once you get the hang of skis, you can have this back." Renata took off as the last words left her mouth. The sleigh was heavy, but glided nicely behind her and she began picking up speed. When she looked behind her, Dusty was up and moving more smoothly, and much more quickly, than he had before.

They weren't making much ground, but they certainly weren't losing any, which would do, given the current, limited stakes. Higher up the mountain, things would get hairy if something happened and they weren't in a pack—really, if something happened things would be hairy anyway.

Renata was in a rhythm and let her mind drift to when she was a girl, out in the bush with her parents and brother. They had a log cabin that seemed to be a million miles from anything and for two weeks every winter and one month every summer, they trekked through the wilds and lived off the land—for the most part; her mother always stashed some canned goods, though they usually came out as a side dish after they'd hunted something down in those first hours. Snowshoe hare was the norm during winter and squirrel was the norm during summer, until something bigger could be brought in. Fruit and fungi were plentiful in the summer, but in the winter, they made pine needle tea and plucked rose hips from trees—their mother would rub the rose hips in her thick leather mitts to clear away the irritating fur.

Those days were long and once the siblings were into their teens, a total bore, but now as Renata glided smoothly, about one hundred pounds of gear strapped to her, she was grateful they'd happened. "If you'd lived a normal childhood you maybe wouldn't have become a wild teen and wouldn't be working this job and wouldn't need to repay your brother's kindness," she mumbled. Still, this wasn't bad and the earlier exhaustion had begun to wane. If nothing else, she was going to have a great sleep tonight.

She heard a noise behind her and glanced back, eyes immediately settling on Dusty's large, lumbering frame. He was doing much better without the sleigh, but he still wasn't great. She suspected that he'd never been on skis before and that he stupidly assumed he could do it because the skilled made it look easy.

"You doing okay?" she said.

He didn't answer, his face was deep red, almost purple, and his eyes looked crazy. He was moving twice as much as was necessary and she wondered what it was they took to get them that kind of energy. She guessed it could be anything, speed maybe—not that she knew what speed was, not really. It had to be something illegal or prescription.

That look forced her to boogie a little faster; she didn't want to be caught out alone with this man, not looking how he did now.

16

The beasts had fanned out, trailing her slowly and steadily. The smallest was only a few inches taller than she was, but the other two were giants. Jenna knew that once they caught her, they'd finish her, and could probably catch her at any time. It was as if they were playing with her—did terror-laced flesh taste different from surprised flesh?

That question drove her to the brink.

Ahead, the skiers stopped for a moment and she pushed all she had into getting close enough while the swish of the skis and the heavy passage of breath buried her screams. But then they were moving again, and faster than before.

"No," she moaned and dropped to her knees.

Heavy footfalls immediately raced toward her from three angles and she scrambled up onto the rocky outcropping. The blue faces had given up their cover and the smallest beast led the pack. Jenna screamed a high, piercing shriek and stabbed her hands into the snowbank leaned against the rock face, scrambling for higher ground. She got her feet beneath her—her hands felt like half-thawed chicken breasts pulled from the freezer.

The growling breaths behind her were so close she thought she could feel the musky backwash of dining on hockey players. But had they had time to eat? Were they simply killers, eyes on punishing interlopers? Was this territorial?

She had no way of knowing and pulled and

kicked, attempting to climb. She got four feet from the ground when ice cracked beneath her right foot and she tumbled. The fall was much greater than to the ground, she was suddenly in an icy cavern. She looked up and a shadow played over the hole. The smaller beast attempted to crawl to her. It got a shoulder and its head through, but was then stopped. It was simply too meaty.

Jenna sat at the bottom, numbed by cold and driven mad by terror, and watched. It grunted and groaned before it pulled out and the biggest head of the trio poked in and growled.

"You can't get me," she whispered and then yelled, "You can't get me!" Her voice echoed behind her in a way that suggested amid the dark icy corridors was a larger space. She imagined another glacial cave and dreaded the possibility of running into more of these things—*not things, fucking yetis!* "You can't get me," she said again and then reeled her hands and knees up under her coat. She dipped her face, chin to chest, and rolled like an egg.

She lay there, shivering, trying to use her breath to heat her when the realization hit that she was as good as dead if she stayed there, as good as if she'd chanced combat against the yetis. If she was going to survive, she needed to get somewhere warmer. Chaotically, she felt around inside her coat and located the purse she'd draped inside and at the back. Her legs sprang down and she sat her butt against the ice. Her arms remained in her coat and she maneuvered the purse down and let it fall to the ice to her right side. Arms back down the sleeves, her shivering hands pawed numbly at the zipper of the purse. Inside were her wallet, a compact, lip liner, mascara, lip gloss, four hair elastics, a half-pack of gum, two tampons, and a red disposable lighter—virtually new.

Her hands nearly vibrated against the spinning wheel and the sparks leapt brightly. Then she got it and the instant bit of heat helped calm her hands. Slowly with the flame lit, she swung around and saw just how lucky it had been that she dropped her purse to her right. Less than a foot left of her, the ice shelf where she sat dropped deeper into the gulley. The gulley was maybe eighteen inches wide, and beyond it was a curious space.

It was almost as if someone had chiselled a ladder into the wall of ice. Too dark to see how high it went, but possibly it was a way out.

"Okay, good," she mumbled, but first thing was first. She let the flame die and then tied her hair back with an elastic. She then pulled her legs and arms within her coat. Her head went to her chin and she tipped sideways. Inside her bulky coat, she lit the lighter and performed a bit of self-care, basking in the quickly mounting heat.

17

Where the rock face ended, Raphael called out for a halt to the movement. It was a quarter after four and they had about twenty minutes of daylight left. Already the steam coming from his mouth lingered longer and the waning sunshine gave everything a blue hue.

"We'll need some wood. Did any of you bring a saw?" Raphael asked, looking beyond the group to where his sister continued her approach, and Dusty a few yards behind her. He hadn't expected her to be pulling the second sleigh, but wasn't surprised. "You know, a saw?"

Sidney smacked his forehead playfully with a mitted hand. "That, my friend, we did not think of."

"Fine. I have one, was hoping there'd be a second." Raphael unshouldered his pack and unzipped it. Immediately his back thanked him. He withdrew the two-body pup tent, the campfire starter bricks, and finally the folded saw. "Anyone not setting up a tent care to hack some—?"

Riccardo snatched the saw. "Me," he said, his breaths heavy and his face sweaty.

Sofia was on her back. "Stupid. Stupid," she said to herself.

Maurice and Sidney worked on their first tent— the second was on the other sleigh. Raphael had his tent flat and was placing the short and flimsy poles into their corners when Renata reached them, gliding in next to the other sleigh. She unlatched and groaned appreciatively when the weight and tension of the hold left her.

Raphael got the tent up and unhooked his sleeping bag from his pack. "How you doing?" he asked.

Renata stretched her back and unslung her own pack—it housed very little by comparison. She unhitched her bag and tossed it to Raphael. "I'm tired and hungry, you?" she said.

"About the same," he said. "Some of our guests seem to have lots of energy." He unrolled Renata's bag into his tent.

"Why am I so stupid?" Sofia mumbled, still lying in the snow.

"She okay?" Renata asked. She had tissue in hand, about to tackle the booger smear crusting her upper lip.

"She always gets the buyer's remorse when she's coming down," Maurice said.

Dusty fell sideways as he attempted to kill his forward momentum. Nobody acknowledged him beyond a glance. Even after he belted a theatrical sigh.

"Coming down from what?" Raphael said, not quite scolding.

"Caffeine. We ate some coffee beans," Sidney said. "Coffee beans are, ah, you know, a great jolt."

"Ah, right," Raphael said, this time his tone hid nothing: he wasn't buying jack about coffee beans or scientific goals.

With the tents up, everyone but Raphael, Renata, and Sofia helped with the wood gathering. There were plenty of trees nearby and a couple were nice and brown. Another had a charred black hole cratering its core from a lightning strike. Dusty had taken to punching at what remained of that tree, and once he had enough cracked, he tore from the edges.

The fire cracked from a foamy brick and was steadily teasing the moisture out of the branches. Within an hour, they'd have a tight and welcoming fire. Raphael yawned and Renata unwillingly mimicked him. Sofia had begun to cry steadily, an icy pool spreading beneath her face where she lay, looking into the fire as if mesmerized.

"How we doing for time?" Renata asked.

"Surprisingly good. Whatever these guys took outweighed their weak skills. If the weather cooperates and the days look like today, we'll be up to the mark by noon or so, day after tomorrow." Raphael had a collapsible pot full of snow, waiting for the fire to get bigger so he could fix everyone's stew packets.

Renata looked at Sofia. "You sure you'll be okay?"

"Yeah," Sofia said. "I just get sad sometimes and need a pick-me-up."

"What kind of pick-me-up?" Renata asked.

"Coke's good. Got some, too. But Sidney says I have to sleep, so the drugs have to be for when we need energy," Sofia said, voice low and emotionless.

"Is that what you took today?" Raphael asked.

"No, Bennies. Wait, Kennies, better than Bennies." Sofia pushed to a sitting position and then scooped a mouthful of snow into her mouth. "At least there's no dog pee," she said around the quickly melting snow.

"Kennies. So that's like speed?" Renata asked Raphael.

"Who cares, whatever gets these scientists up the mountain." Raphael put a bit of teasing on the word scientist.

Renata turned back to Sofia and was about to ask if they were really scientists, but Sidney had stepped within earshot and it no longer felt like a time to speak candidly. The fire grew bigger and hotter as the branches caught. Raphael heated the water to close enough to boiling that he couldn't wait anymore and everyone filled a collapsible cup with soup. Raphael and Renata ate ravenously while the others seemed to force it down. When the Le Page siblings started into the high-calorie chocolate bars, the others accepted chunks because chocolate was chocolate, but generally didn't seem hungry.

"How's dumping work here?" Dusty said.

Renata frowned and grimaced, but Raphael said, "Best option is to find a log and sit over the edge. If you can't find a log, take a shovel and dig a hole to squat over." He rooted into his pack and came up with environmentally friendly toilet paper. "Don't over use, only have two rolls for the whole trip."

Maurice, who hadn't said anything in hours started to laugh and said, "Just pull your ass around over the snow like some mutt with the worms."

Riccardo found this especially funny and joined in laughing; the sound echoed down the mountain and came back like a ghost.

18

Jenna had killed her lighter, but remained in her egg of warmth until coolness reigned anew. She couldn't waste all the fluid, but it was tough not to relight and bask in the slight comfort it offered.

Instead, she lifted her head and looked up to the hole she'd come through. Like a broken skylight. The moon shined in, seemingly bringing the frosty air in along with it. She listened, her ears aflame at the suddenness of the temperature change—her ears hadn't wanted to warm up in the first place, but had finally acquiesced. She had no idea how long she'd been down here, but silently thanked her father for having no idea about her size of coat. If it hadn't looked so cute on her, like she'd borrowed her boyfriend's letterman jacket or something, she would've taken it back. Now it had saved her life.

"Maybe," she said and pushed her legs out. Arms back in her sleeves, hands bent like claws hidden beneath elastic at the wrists of the coat, she stepped over the crevice. Most of the cavern was full dark, but she saw enough of the makeshift ladder to get a feel. "Please, God, don't take me into a cave full of those…yetis."

How do yetis exist even?

She pulled her weight and quickly learned she had to put bare fingers against the slick, icy holds. From the hole behind her, one of the beasts huffed and snorted, as if again attempting to push into her cavern. Fine, let them be stupid. She continued climbing. To her surprise and almost detriment, the rise topped out at about nine feet. She pushed down and kept her boots working in the holds even as her hips were above the edge. She fell forward after the next step, thumping hard against more ice, but also stone.

A trickle of water ran from the stone below the ice and she dipped her hand, the sound suddenly drawing out her thirst. She sipped two mouthfuls from her palm and then shoved that hand down the front of her pants. The depth of the cold of that stream was incredible; it sank into her bones. With her other hand, she reached into her pocket for the lighter.

The flame illuminated an ascending shaft through rock, high enough that she could crouch-walk, at least for as far as the firelight reached. She pocketed the light and withdrew her other hand from her pants. She pushed to her knees and then to her feet. Slowly, she plodded up the steep slope with her hands in her pockets. Feeling relatively safe from immediate death, she thought of Connor and her destroyed escape plan. She totally now wished she hadn't gone against the biggest no-no in Le Sommet's rulebook.

Still, she didn't necessarily feel stupid about it; if it had worked, it would've changed her life. A small sob hitched in her throat when she realized it had already changed her life, might've been the inciting incident that led to her demise.

"Fuck," she whispered and then reached for her lighter. She'd been walking for several minutes already.

The glow cast no longer banked. The ice was mostly gone but for in the gully with the running stream. That, of course, didn't mean it was any warmer. Rock everywhere and it seemed never ending. She pocketed the lighter once again and continued walking. She tried to think warm thoughts, which led to thoughts of food. She imagined the magically greasy square pizza from the Pizza Delight in the town where she grew up. It was what they fed the students at her elementary school on pizza days and it was what they ordered when the group sat around hungover years later.

What she wouldn't do for just a corner of that pizza…

For any food, really.

Time passed, but she had no idea of knowing how quickly. Her phone had fallen with Connor and Leon's phones. She hadn't had a watch since the Timex her mother had bought her as a Christmas gift, back in the ninth grade. Watches were jewelry and step-counters nowadays, totally useless to Jenna out there in the real world, and mostly useless here.

Knowing the time would only suggest knowing when she might get so exhausted that she'd fall down and die. And she felt like she'd been walking for hours now, the drip of the water finding the ice patch was well out of earshot. Her legs suddenly felt as if they'd give way and she'd sink, tumble back with the water, and die in that icy chamber.

"Nice thought," she said and then her face bumped against stone.

She reached into her pocket for the lighter and discovered a wall before her, though it didn't reach all the way to the floor. She bent lower, and when that didn't give her a proper sightline, she dropped to her knees.

Snow. And something else, something she didn't dare believe. She palmed the lighter and began crawling, racing beneath the wall. The stone under her was dusty and the edges grated against her uncomfortably, but she made it through. A pine needle touched her face and she nearly screamed—equal parts terror and glee, because what if that wasn't a huge pile of pine boughs and sticks…but oh Lord, it had certainly looked like that.

Once the rest of the way through, she lit the lighter. It had to be a forgotten animal den. The pine boughs were brown and most of the needles had fallen, making a great mound—suggesting they'd been refilled often—there were sticks, a huge pile of them, there were also other items, ones that didn't fit with the animal den assumption.

Wooden snowshoes sat on the floor, halfway buried in pine needles. She crawled further and discovered the small stack of newspapers, the little sticker on the corner addressed to Le Sommet, the date from only a year ago. A set of camping cookware. Cans of peaches! Cans of corn! Two cans of ham! Jenna spun and drank in the rest of the cave. In the back corner, next to a boulder blocking the view from where she'd entered, was a fire pit.

"Thank you, God," she said and got busy; building the first campfire she'd ever built, then muscling open the peaches with an old-timey can opener only to find a block of ice inside. She set that can next to the fire and dug into a can of ham.

The meat was dry and dropped from the container like a puck, still so frozen that she had to bite from the edge as she would from a sandwich.

Even with the fire going, she shivered. Without her conscious of it, her eyes volleyed between the hole where the heat was escaping to the wall of snow blocking what she assumed was the actual entrance—the front door. Minutes passed and she could no longer eat, having to keep her entire body close to the fire. The cold had totally buried itself beneath her skin and she imagined never being warm again, and then it hit her.

Sixteen minutes later, the cave became toasty—relatively toasty—after she'd relocated enough snow to block most of the tunnel that led her there. She tried not to think about what came next or who put all that stuff in the cave and simply enjoyed surviving; for now.

19

Morning came upon the group hard and fast. Raphael and Renata were groggy, but after some chocolate, a power bar, and a cup of thick coffee, they were ready to go. The others were not so focused at first. All looked as if they'd hardly slept. Dusty, being the least in shape, looked like he might call it quits.

Raphael and Renata stepped away to let pressure off their internal plumbing and by the time they got back, the group was wide awake, almost thrumming by comparison. Renata looked at her brother and he shrugged again. They were paid to get these people up the mountain, not worry that Riccardo and Sofia still had coke clung to the edges of their nostrils.

All strapped their skis and poles to their packs; for Raphael and Renata this meant to their backs, while the others split the weight between the two sleighs. Maurice and Sidney were on sleigh duty to start, and Raphael guessed one of them would be at it for most of the day—even with their pick-me-up, Dusty was flagging. After about an hour, he sat down and Sofia—though not impressed—came to his aid. He ate what she gave him and the group carried on.

"He'll catch up," Sidney said, grinning, pallor gone yellow. He looked downright ghoulish. "He's a big guy, needs a bigger break."

"I don't know," Raphael said.

"Just fucking go!" Dusty said, his voice

cracking at the tail of the demand.

The group paid a few more seconds of interest to the big lump in the snow. He looked like he might never move again.

"Maybe he should go back down the mountain," Renata said. "Much easier going down."

"Fuck off. I'll be fine, just give me a bit." Dusty had his eyes closed and his chin on his chest.

"Please, do let us continue," Sidney said.

Raphael shrugged once more and started up the steepest part of the trek. The snow crunched beneath them and winter birds watched from the trees dotting the mountain. Within the hour, Dusty was just a speck behind them, but he'd gotten up and was moving in the right direction.

"He's coming," Raphael said.

Renata looked back and huffed out a big, relieved breath. The others didn't seem to care as much, as if they had all the faith in the world that he'd make it to his feet and follow them eventually.

By the second hour, Dusty was an ant behind them, but still moving. They stopped for coffee and chocolate, watching the slow labor of his movements. After another hour, the worst of it was behind them—at least until the final push up—and they crested a hill.

"Should we wait?" Renata said.

They wouldn't be able to see him until he crested that hill and that might be hours away.

"Have to put skis on now or right over there," Raphael said, pointing to where a new wall of rock jutted out and they'd have to cross back in the opposite direction from their first use of the skis.

"Might as well do it now," Sidney said, peering over the crest at Dusty. "It looks like he's got a burst of energy now."

Everyone else leaned out to see and it did seem as if Dusty was suddenly boogying, at least moving his arms a lot; from that far away it was difficult to tell if it did him any good.

"Right, that'll do," Raphael said and unshouldered his pack.

"And if he's not here by the time we start moving," Sidney lifted his arms, palms up as he spoke, "we can draw an arrow in the snow, capeesh?"

20

Kevin Sheenan was an expert on all things unorthodox and extraordinary when it came to animal life on Earth, as well as those lifeforms from the great beyond who'd come to visit Earth. In 1999, he feared the collapse of civilization and trained in survival tactics. He became an outdoorsman. He became a hunter. He used stealth and patience as his prime tools.

When the computers didn't crash, Kevin's attentions shifted back to Animalia and the truths the common world refused to acknowledge. That refusal sparked the fuse that exploded his life. He turned his back on his obligations—a wife, a home, his job—and sought to build an undeniable case around an obsession.

Years passed and he delved deeper into the worlds of cryptids until his focus settled on something so common that it couldn't be ignored: the sasquatch. On nearly every continent and noted throughout all of written history, the giant man-like beast dwelled on the periphery like a ghost.

The chase took him all over the world until his humanity devolved to the point where he could no longer function amongst people and preferred to live amongst beasts. Le Sommet and the mountain beneath it were perfect. He'd found trace evidence of yetis in the valley on the far side of the first peak, and when he needed to, he could sneak down to civilization and steal anything he wanted.

For two years he set up caches in caves; places and food sources he could use in a pinch, and why? Because he'd seen the beasts, finally, up close and personal. He'd seen the beasts and had barely escaped with his life. They were omnivores, but hungered fresh, hot flesh most of all.

Even with the scare, Kevin did not flee the mountain. Instead, he dug deeper, finding more safe spots, creating more caches. For months, he didn't glimpse the incredible beasts again, not until a great crash rocked the quiet of the mountain. This brought beasts—already much closer to Kevin than he'd realized—out of hiding. He'd watched through stolen binoculars as the family of yetis devoured the human remains resulting from the helicopter crash.

Unlike every other time he'd seen them on the mountaintop, they crossed down, heading for the civilized side and eventually, Le Sommet. This put him in a strange position; should he warn people? Or, should he just let nature take its course?

If he warned people, they'd call him crazy, right until the moment the beasts tore them limb from limb. But, if he simply watched it happen, he wouldn't be the one to finally reveal unequivocal proof that at least one form of the sasquatch mythology was true.

This was a tough enough decision that he trailed the beasts as they carefully moved downhill. He remained close by while the four deaths occurred and then watched the woman escape and send the beasts backward on their trek, now heading away from collective humanity. The woman had disappeared and Kevin then recognized the back entrance to one of his caches, and wondered if she'd found her way to his things. This trespass didn't exactly make him mad, but it did feel like a slight against him.

The beasts remained by the opening they'd never fit through for many hours before they sniffed out a new trail to follow. Kevin had glimpsed the group just prior to when the second set of victims entered the glacial cave, but they'd been headed safely away from the action. Or what seemed like safety at the time, now, he saw they were being hunted.

"To intervene or to observe?" he asked the face he'd painted on the end of his right mitten.

The mitten answered, "Don't do anything you might regret."

Kevin nodded and trailed, keeping one eye on the progress up the mountain and the other on the yetis.

21

The drugs had hit Dusty little by little. It wasn't until he felt utterly alone—and suddenly more than a hint paranoid—that the chemicals fully took root. He felt like he could run, almost. A voice inside warned him that running was how he'd burnout and be left with no gas in the tank and no way to keep going, no way to claim his rightful portion of the dough.

Christ, when this was all over, he was going to Italy. His great grandmother had come from there and according to his grandmother—rest her soul— the Volpe name harbored great respect and even some fear. He'd then keep going, see all those little countries, and find the roots of his mother's side, maybe even bring her along for the ride. Dusty had never felt a great fit in North America, nor in any of the dozens of cities he'd lived in. South America was too hot, as were all those little islands floating in-between. But with his criminal record, he'd never been able to go to Europe before now—this phony passport cost a bundle and wasn't built to last. With his chunk of that cash, he could grease any palm needing greased and never again worry about his past.

A sound that came aside from the thump and swish of his snowshoes and the rush of his heavy breaths pulled Dusty from his thoughts and he looked over one shoulder and then the other. He shook his head, blinking. The snow, it moved up and then flopped back down.

"Seeing things," he said.

The trek resumed and Dusty tried to imagine what would cause the snow to move and then he asked himself just how high was he? He'd slept maybe an hour the night before. He'd ingested three prescription servings of methamphetamine and had taken a total of three bumps of cocaine.

"Imagining it," he said beneath harsh breaths.

Still…he glanced back and saw the same kind of movement. This time he stopped and stared at the spot where the snow had seemed to move. His eyes suddenly became incredibly dry and he bent to grab some snow. The change in angle made the light play off the shadows differently.

Dusty drank it in; that mid-dark shadow was an animalistic face and those two darker shadows were dull black eyes.

"Yo," he whispered. More movement in the snow, this time to his right; a bigger face, and hands, and… "Fur?" The math all came together and Dusty popped upright and started running. "There's abominable snowmans! Abominable snowmans!"

When he glanced back, the smallest one was up and had forgone its stealth. It ran; its feet like natural snowshoes over the crunchy floor. Dusty was losing ground and too intent on watching behind him to remain diligent of his steps. He crossed the snowshoes and tumbled flat. One foot came free of the clumsy shoe and he pushed upright. His first step was fine, his second sunk several inches. The beast's breath was upon him, right there tickling the space on his neck where his collar didn't quite reach his cotton beanie. He felt inside his coat for the long knife. They had two rifles for when it came time to deal with the guides, but those were packed and hidden in the sleighs.

He flopped forward into the snow, spinning as he did so, to face the beast. The knife came out and he stabbed at the leaping creature, but the plastic sheath remained over the blade and the yeti absorbed the blow and then rolled away with a surprised cry.

Dusty's arm took the weight of the beast poorly and pain thrummed up from his wrist. Limply, he worked at removing the sheath, swinging his good arm out straight once he got it. The beast had leapt again and lukewarm blood spilled onto Dusty. The beast roared against Dusty's chest a half-second before it sank its incredible teeth and the sound of his snapped chest plate rang over the mountainside like a dinner bell.

The bigger beasts joined in and Dusty remained alive as they tore him apart, bringing his flesh, muscles, and organs to their mouths. The squelching and slurping seemed impossibly loud and his mind flittered: this was a stadium show; on the big screen the beasts ate him and 80,000 fans watched in silence as the massive speakers carried the meal's report with crystal clear sound. The last thing he saw was the medium face and the medium hands take out his heart. Thankfully, he died before he saw the thing devour the precious muscle.

22

The wind began to pick up some, pushing down from the mountaintop. It killed the limited chatter that had gone on between the members of the group up until then. Raphael lifted his hood, tightening the face-hole by the nibs on the elastic tethers, and fell into a zone. This was one of his happy places; the steady exertion and the resulting chemical reaction. Loving it was how he became a national champion, how he came to compete on the international stage—had it not been for the Swedes, Finns, and Norwegians, the same countries in just about every version of his event and every year, he'd have medalled. He smiled, recalling how a Norwegian put an arm around Raphael's shoulder, two golds dangling from his neck, and said, "It's not your fault, we're born on skis."

His stomach rumbled and he took a second to gauge the distance until they'd reach the second to last leg. Guessing, they were an hour from the next stop; this was the best scenario, timing-wise anyway. He took a deep breath and looked over his shoulder, counting heads. He slowed, giving Sofia a chance to decrease her wayward kicks before he came to a stop. He counted approaching bodies and Dusty hadn't yet caught them.

"Dusty's just fat and slow, come on," Sofia said before Raphael had a chance to say anything.

She was visibly zooming, and from experience, Raphael understood that the crash came hard and fast. Still, he was in charge. "Hey, any sign of Dusty back there?" he shouted.

Sidney turned and shouted, "Dusty looking fine back there?"

Riccardo turned, as did Renata. She didn't see Dusty, but Riccardo called up, "He's coming, keep going!"

Sofia gave Raphael a sickly grin and he shrugged. He put the hood back over his head and pushed onward. If nothing else, he could force a slightly extended lunch period, to hell with the *scientists* and what they wanted, let them take more uppers, let them get finicky and bitchy. This was his show. They'd never make it to the top without him.

"But why?" he said, suddenly concerned about the mystery that drove them. It had to be something major, and what waited for them at that GPS location? And what happened to him and Renata once they got to the top? He sighed. "Fuck."

23

Jenna awoke coughing. The smoke had finally filled the cave, threatening to take her refuge and turn it into a deathtrap. She pushed to her knees and squinted at the wall of snow. Between bouts of sleeping and waking, she'd considered that wall of snow and tried to imagine just how deep it might be. Now she had to find out.

She picked up one of the old, wooden snowshoes. It was shaped like a tennis racket, even had a long handle where the tines that crossed it wrapped the framework together. She crawled to the snow wall, held her breath, and closed her eyes. She poked the long skinny end high as she could reach from her knees and kept pushing. It took only seconds before a cool draft began wafting in.

Part of her wanted to break down the snow wall, get busy figuring out what came next, but she decided against it. She wanted to rest more, eat more peaches.

She dropped back down and dug a handful of icy snow from the wall and put it in her mouth. The coolness soothed her irritated throat and she lay, waiting for a time when the atmosphere might not hurt her eyes. She rested and…she slipped back into consciousness without realizing she'd again slept. The air was frosty and clean, the campfire was nothing but embers. She got busy rebuilding her heat source. It took very little effort.

She grabbed the peach can she'd licked from the

night before and fingered the slushy liquid, breaking up the last of the ice surrounding the frozen chunks of fruit. A piece big enough to halfway fill her mouth went in, and she sucked; so cold that it hurt her teeth, and yet, she dared not spit it out. She worked it around with her tongue so it didn't press against any one tooth for too long. After a minute, she risked a bite and found her teeth sinking, though not all the way through. An ache stung deep beneath her gums but she forced herself, adding to the fire, making it hot, hot, hot, as if that would make the cold, cold, cold in her mouth more bearable.

As she focused on the fruit and the fire, a not-so-distant sound fought for her attention. She made the space of her mouth big enough to cradle the semi-chewed peach without letting it touch her fuzzy teeth. Her hands held the sticks she'd just then been using to stoke the fire. Her right ear tilted up to the hole she'd carved.

People talking.

One voice almost certainly sounded like Raphael Le Page, the cute ski instructor and sister to her former co-worker, Renata Le Page. She crunched down hard, trying to defeat the frozen peach so that she could yell out—never did it cross her mind to spit.

More voices joined the first and then a swishing sound began trailing away from her cave. She got the fruit swallowed and began shouting, "Hey! Hey, I'm in here!" over and over. She began stabbing at the snow wall—much of the interior had gone to ice thanks to the campfire—still shouting. Poking a hole was not the same as carving her way out. She stabbed and slashed, channeling her inner Jason Voorhees, but finding none of the skill.

Minutes raced by and she went manic, thrashing and growling, shouting at the wall to let her go. Eventually, she understood, the cave opening was more like an S than the inviting yawn of an O. Where she'd pocked originally was sheer luck, where she'd clawed and cut afterward was mostly against solid stone.

By the time she solved this puzzle and had daylight shining in, she had to sit a minute and catch her breath. She dropped all the sticks and newspaper into the fire pit and picked up the frozen meat she'd been chewing on. It had gone much softer, making it much grosser, but she chewed and swallowed nonetheless. When she began gagging, she shovelled peach slush into her mouth.

The heat from the fire had her squinting as she grabbed for snow to wash her hands. The cold bit, but the fire quickly warmed and dried. She pocketed an unopened can of ham and got to investigating the snowshoes. She was light, and maybe she could run on whatever trail those people she'd heard had left, but then again, maybe not. She shoved the snowshoes outside and then crawled free from the cave, her hands cold and wet all over again.

Not twenty feet from the cave was a fresh-packed ski trail. She walked, feet every third step, until on the trail. There, she stood and shuffled, not falling through. She couldn't see the people, but knew the direction by ear.

"To hell with it," she said and tossed the old snowshoes away—they had to weigh ten pounds each. She got to jogging, the canned ham bouncing uncomfortably in her loose jacket pocket. Sometimes her foot fell through, but mostly, she was doing okay, which said a lot, given her mental state right then.

24

Sofia kept Raphael's speed up until it was time to stop for lunch and re-don the snowshoes. After, they'd make it halfway up the final piece and then stop for the night, ahead of schedule. Raphael was exhausted and finally truly understood the power of amphetamines.

Maurice plunked down next to the others when he arrived. He was pale and his jaw seemed to move with a mind of its own. He hadn't slept at all the night before and the drugs were starting to cloud things for him. The sound of gliding across snow had come to sound like a car crash localized in his mind. Money or no money, he wished he'd just stayed home.

"Chocolate?" Renata asked, holding out a foil wrapped bar.

The scent oozed out with pink tendrils and danced into Maurice's nose and down his throat, tickling his uvula until he gagged and began vomiting in the snow next to him. Riccardo laughed, but it was desperate, totally lacking humor.

"Get away!" Maurice said and then rolled, his cheek pressing into the chunky, acidic liquid that had melted a hole through the snow. "Leave me!"

"Jesus," Sofia said, grimacing widely enough to show her top row of teeth between very chapped lips. "That's gonna be me. I know it. I'm so stupid, why do I always do stupid shit?"

"Maybe you need some sugar," Riccardo said,

as if the drugs remained a secret.

"That's it, another dumb decision," Sofia said. She was slumped like a doll.

Raphael puffed out a breath that didn't even steam as the breeze stole it before it had the chance. Rather than worry about these people and the chemical reactions happening inside them, he got busy eating his lunch. Renata did not settle for the distraction as simply.

"What if he gets worse?" she whispered.

Raphael looked at Maurice as he chewed. "We could stop here for the day. We'd get to the top by supper tomorrow."

Sofia snorted, snapping her head straight back from the packet she held in her little pink hand. She blinked at Raphael and Renata, then stared hard.

"What?" Renata said.

"Is that real?" she said, pointing up the mountain.

Sidney clicked his tongue and watched, the first to know exactly what he looked at. The cyclone of one hundred Euro bills was so impossibly out of place that it couldn't be…unless knowing the truth, knowing differently.

"I say, we keep this train chugging along. Maurice can keep a tent for when Dusty comes up, if he's out of energy too." Sidney watched the money—about two grand—flitter closer and closer.

"Is that cash?" Renata said, face contorted in confusion.

Raphael lifted an eyebrow at Sidney, then Riccardo, then Sofia, and finally Maurice. He came back to Sidney who'd begun looking back at him.

"Yes, we'll move," he said.

"And leave him? What's the money from?" Renata said.

Sofia popped to her feet and tried to chase down the bills, but her feet sank up to her thighs. She turned, laughing, manic, "Oh yeah!"

"Shoes on," Riccardo said.

"Shoes on," Sidney repeated.

"We're just leaving him? What the hell?" Renata said.

Raphael leaned in tight to his sister, breathing chocolate breath against her cheek. "These people are gangsters. These people are here for money that is somehow on the mountain. These people mean business. These people are in charge." He put his hand on Renata's arm and squeezed. "Play along with them until we reach the top."

The others were busy with snowshoes and uppers. Raphael pulled more chocolate from his pack as he straightened up, pretending to be very concerned with it. Renata hadn't said anything back just yet, but he knew she would. She was good for thinking a minute before reacting—when she was away from bad influences anyway. Even when they were kids and she was about to have a meltdown, she took a pause and calibrated her argument—even when it turned out insane. When she was in trouble, she took a breath and exhaled her defense. When someone tested her into her teens, the pauses were shorter and the retorts more curt, but there was always a moment of thought.

"We can ski down in a day, easy, if we're not babysitting," she whispered, reaching across to snatch away the chocolate bar. "They'll never keep up."

Raphael nodded gently. He pulled the snowshoes from his pack and attached them to his feet. He leaned over. "I'll call someone if I get a chance," he whispered. It was doubtful anyone else had the satellite attachment on their phone. He stood, affixed his skis and poles to his pack, and nodded again, this time to Sidney.

Renata again brought up the rear. Riccardo had relinquished pulling the fuller of the two sleighs and Sidney took over. Sofia was bouncy, lithe, but looked sickly, like a walking dead woman.

25

Jenna got the hang of moving steadily without snowshoes. In the beginning, things went great, but then patches formed, and the snow was much deeper fifteen-hundred feet up the mountain. She tried to remember high school gym classes when they'd gone out on skis and snowshoes, while never forgetting that somewhere behind her were giant beasts. Despite being clunky, she wished she'd kept those old things. Often she considered veering off the path and striking off down the hill, but she didn't dare. If she found people, they could call for help or something. Something. Maybe they could be meals for the beasts and she could manage another escape, hell, maybe they had a way to get a helicopter and she could be on the ground an hour or two after meeting up with them.

She could move away from the mountain. If she could just get to safety, she'd stop with the laziness and the conniving. She'd go back to school and become something herself instead of trying to leech off somebody famous…but being Mrs. Connor Murray would've been sweet, and not just because of the money and the fame and the looks; he seemed like a nice enough guy.

She groaned, "Connor," and tried to pick up her pace.

She looked over her shoulder regularly, but saw nothing coming for her, but the lack of blue faces and hands, that white fur, had her paranoid. It gave her imagination space to grow yetis from snowy lumps and gray shadows. They'd rise up and begin the chase, but this time she had no snowmobile or lucky tunnel.

"Stop," she said under her labored breaths.

She was freaking herself out unnecessarily. Head down, eyes on the trail, she pushed onward until the trail suddenly stopped and in the snow before her was a man and a scuffed aluminum sleigh. A one-hundred Euro bill was in his mitted hand and according to the angle and the stillness, acquiring this cash might've been the last thing he'd done.

"Hello? Are you—?" she said before the man sat up.

His eyes were bloodshot and vomit rimmed his mouth like boot-leather-brown clown paint. He smacked his mouth and lifted the mitted hand not holding the cash.

"Where's Dusty?" he said and then, "Want it? I can't."

Naturally, like when someone waves and the only recourse is waving back, Jenna reached out her cold pink hand from within the sleeve of her jacket. The man, Maurice, dropped a single white pill. Moisture had roughened it up around the edges.

"Do you have a phone?" she said, looking at the pill, thinking even as bad as this man was, pills were good, helpful. "Is this Tylenol?" She knew it wasn't, but she felt awfully tired and sore; stopping to chat only compounded that.

"Tylenol?" Maurice said.

"Do you have a phone?" Jenna said, and then

before she knew what her hand was doing, the pill went into her mouth and when she tried to swallow, it got stuck at the back of her tongue. She gagged and bent, taking up a handful of snow to wash the thing down.

"Guy up there, he's got a phone."

Jenna blinked away tears from gagging and looked up the mountain. Way up there was a small pack of people. "It's Renata, right? And her brother?"

"Who are you? Police?" Maurice said and suddenly lurched forward and pitched his body to the sleigh.

Jenna tumbled back, dropping the canned ham. Her heart immediately began to race and she played through the possibilities of what might be strapped to that sleigh.

"Fucking police," Maurice said, slurring it, as if he'd had a stroke.

"No, I'm not," Jenna said and began kicking— on the ground next to a pack were two aluminum snowshoes. If she had to go up to get to the phone, and more than likely a ride off the goddamned mountain, a pack and some lightweight snowshoes weren't going to hurt her chances.

"Sidney! Sidney, we got trouble," Maurice shouted and began tugging at something long and skinny, wrapped in a white bath towel with the words LE SOMMET embroidered along the ends.

Jenna didn't wait to see if that thing that was shaped like a rifle was really a rifle. She kicked to her feet and ran, snatching the pack not affixed to the sleigh, and then one snowshoe, and then the other, before scrambling to a big rock. She got behind the rock and waited.

"What the fuck?" Maurice said after a few moments.

Jenna crouched and shouldered the pack. She then stepped into the shoes and affixed the sturdy rubber straps over her boots.

Maurice began coughing hard enough to lead to his vomiting again and Jenna took her chance. The guy was totally out of it—*and you accepted a pill from him!* She broke in an ambling attempt at running.

"Sidney!" Maurice shouted. He fired once, missing Jenna by about fifteen feet.

Her heart began pounding harder and terror filled her muscles with adrenaline. She dove behind another rock, and waited. And waited. And waited.

"Where's my money? Gonna buy a boat," Maurice said and then spat.

Jenna waited a little while longer until, as if flipping a switch, her body refused to let her sit there. She had to move. The first impulse was to go back and kick the man so he couldn't shoot her, but that was insane. The second impulse was followed and had her hurrying as best she could up the mountain until the man down there left her mind and she again wondered about that pill.

Because it was excellent.

Amazing.

She could run until the end of time.

26

The cluster of trees hid the hovel Kevin had built six, maybe seven, months earlier. The snow never left the mountain that high up, and he'd tunneled twenty feet preceding, creating a vent shaft to house the smoke he created. The heat had iced the tunnel and interior walls, and Kevin had polished the surfaces, both inside and outside, to create a pane of glass. Branches obscured the ice window enough that he felt safe watching through his binoculars as the woman approached the man who had been left behind by the group heading for the peak—a place he hadn't been since the yetis chased him down.

The woman stole the man's snowshoes and pack and then sought cover. He wondered what propelled her higher—like the damsel booting it upstairs in a slasher flick. The man on the ground didn't look well at all, but he was moving, and then he took a shot with a fine-looking rifle.

"Holy," Kevin said, looking at the face on his mitt.

Minutes passed while Kevin and his mitten watched the curious scene. The woman took off and the man fell to his side. It was almost as if he'd been shot, but only one report echoed over the mountainside.

The binoculars went down and Kevin paused in thought. Something seriously fishy was going on. He at first wondered if these people were yeti hunters, and then if they were simply adventurers who'd picked an unexpectedly dangerous mountain that should've been fairly routine.

"What do you think?" he asked the mitten; that face simply stared back at him.

From his pocket, Kevin withdrew a chunk of salted rabbit meat with the hand not wearing a mitten and slipped it into his mouth. He slurped as he chewed gently, softening the meat. The binoculars went back to his eyes and instantly, he caught motion. Three moving lumps. He stopped chewing and let the meat dangle and saliva run from the corner of his mouth.

The man lifted the rifle from where he sat and scanned the world around him.

Kevin whispered, "If he squints, he'll see them," around the chunk of meat.

The beasts seemed to understand what a rifle did, or at least understood they needed to be wary of this figure. The lumps trailed from in front of the man to his sides, working to get in behind him.

"Oops," Kevin said.

The juvenile beast wasn't quite as efficient and the motion was so visible that even this overwrought man saw it. The man fired a round, missing by less than a foot. This was enough to enrage the mother yeti; it leapt. The man fired again, into the air, as claws raked at his chest, releasing a great puff of steam and a rattle crackle as ribs and chest plate snapped. Blood oozed into the snow, haloing a massive swatch of pink.

The father of the threesome stood by, idly watching as organs were torn from the body cavity and bones were tossed in the air. The juvenile leapt up like a dog and caught one of the larger bones, and was already chewing away muscle and gristle as it dropped back to the snow. The mother bit down on the dead man's neck, beheading the body. It spat and the head rolled to the big male. He casually picked it up and began carving the skull like a can opener; using a single claw. The cranium popped free and spun in the snow, sprinklering a showing of red droplets in an ovular pattern. In the beast's palm, the brain looked so utterly useless, as if no fantastical pulses had ever gone on within, no dreams, or goals, or passions. This was a dead food thing, like an overlarge walnut.

The meat fell from Kevin's mouth as the beast bit into the brain. He shivered and lowered the binoculars. The meat had fallen next to the fire. He wiped it in the snow and re-inserted it between his teeth. "Five second rule," he said.

The meal took several minutes and once through, the trio began digging into the man's belongings. They seemed to find nothing of use and they ambled off emptyhanded, plopping down into the crunchy snow only fifteen yards from the trail. What came next was maybe his favorite discovery about the beasts.

Once secured, they huddled in tighter and began shaking their fur. The snow that had clung to them rose and filled in the cracks around them. Within seconds, there were no shadows, indentations, or mounds. The surface was smooth and the beasts were one with the snow.

Kevin lowered the binoculars again and got to

thinking. It might be time to announce to the world that yetis exist, and that he had proof. With his knowledge of their actions and traits, the way they moved and how they hid themselves, he'd have no trouble leading a posse to them. And what if he saved this group from the beasts? He'd be a hero on top of everything else.

"Thinking smart, Kevy Fresh," he said—the name an old joke, something from his youthful days in New Jersey when his mind was far from monsters and focused instead on rhyming over beatbox.

The mitten seemed to nod at him. Yes, this was a good plan.

He stomped out the remains of his small campfire. He then dug his way out of the hovel and crept further up the mountain, taking it slow—wouldn't pay for the beasts to find him now, though they always took a little time to digest their food. Once he reached a good enough distance, he picked up speed, though wasn't moving as quickly as the group. He had six more hideouts in the general area between where he was and the top. Surely one would give him a good enough view to make a final, life-changing decision.

27

"Long and hard is the way that up the mountain leads to retirement," Sidney said between grunted breaths.

They were coming onto a particularly useful place on the mountain; a ledge of sorts with high rock on one side and trees on the other and directly in front. Here was where Raphael had a mind to stop for the day, and with sundown only a half hour away, he was about to suggest it—only suggest it, given that he'd discovered he wasn't really in charge. The coverage offered up a nice reprieve from the wind, but it also carried their voices and Raphael wanted nothing to do with whatever Sidney was talking about.

"So, uh, this is where I had planned to camp," Raphael said over his shoulder as he crested the ledge. Snow had drifted in, but it would take only a minute or two with the collapsible shovels to clear sufficient space. "How's everybody feeling?"

Sidney stopped and cleared his throat. His eyes grew wide, as if he'd awakened from a strange dream. Sofia came up behind him, charging along until she tripped and toppled.

"What the fuck!" she shouted, snow speckling her face.

"He wants to stop," Sidney said.

Riccardo reached them, began nodding immediately. He was green and sweaty, snot glistened down onto his lips. "Yes. Yes," he said.

"How're you so tired?" Sofia said, trying to stand.

Renata caught up and said nothing. She'd spent the afternoon planning an escape, and now that she was close to Raphael, it's all she thought about. These people threw away friends, what would they do to her and her brother?

"Quiet," Sidney said. "This is where we stop for the day." He forced a smile to his face and looked *into* Raphael.

Raphael shivered. Then shrugged. His pack came down in a swoop and he retrieved a shovel that had been strapped to the side.

"What are you doing?" Sofia said, watching Raphael. "You ever even a shovel before?"

Raphael didn't spare a thought for the woman. In minutes, maybe an hour, maybe more, but soon, she'd crash. Tears would flow and the self-deprecation would continue through much of the night. Nothing she said was worth much until she sobered up and started confessing; perhaps mumbling some tidbit that would make life easier once they got away. Then again, maybe he and Renata were both overreacting.

"Give me that," Sofia said, taking two steps and falling again. This time she reefed at the straps of her snowshoes. "Goddamn fucking things!"

"It would behoove you to chill out, girly," Sidney said.

"Go fuck yourself, you wannabe gang—"

Sofia got no more words out before Sidney leapt onto her back and shoved her face into the snow. He grunted and clenched his teeth as he pressed. Her arms and legs flailed. Riccardo seemed not at all alarmed from where he sat like a lump a few feet away. Raphael grabbed Sidney's shoulder and tugged, but the man had amphetamine strength, was like a bull.

And if it wasn't for his own decision, Sidney would've finished Sofia there, but he let her up. She broke the snowy surface as if she'd been drowning and gasped for breath. Tears slipped down her cheeks amid the melting snow. Blood stood out in stark contrast from the seven places that her lips had cracked.

"Fuck you, you're not getting another—Hey!"

Sidney bent over Sofia, digging into her pockets. She slammed at his back and he shoved her to the snow anew. In his hand were the two baggies, frozen together from the perspiration and condensation within her pocket.

"Another what, you low rate whore?" he said.

Everyone else was silent.

"You wouldn't," Sofia said, eyeing the drugs Sidney had cocked behind his head, ready to pitch down the mountain. "You need them as much as I do."

"We reach the top after a half-day tomorrow?" Sidney said, mouth pointed at Raphael, eyes pinned on Sofia.

"That's right," Raphael said.

"And the trip down is significantly easier?" Sidney said.

"Yes," Raphael said.

"I can do a half-day and then an easy day or two to follow, how about you?" Sidney said and pitched the packets. Once they reached the lip of the ledge, a gust of wind picked them up and carried them several yards, disappearing them in the seemingly forever white on white on white.

"Suck my dick," Sofia said.

Sidney huffed and then fell back. In the silence following, Raphael and Renata got busy clearing a space for the tents and a campfire. Both wanted to converse, but neither dared.

"Hoo, it's raining cash," Sidney said and plucked a one hundred Euro bill from the air that had been tumble-weeding down the mountainside.

28

The fire was little match for the coolness that high up. Raphael and Renata huddled in tight, almost as tight as Sofia and Riccardo. Sidney had his boots almost in the coals and embers. After a supper of protein bars and double mugs of hot chocolate, all retreated to their tents in an attempt to preserve heat.

"Have you tried to call anybody yet?" Renata asked.

Raphael had only just zipped the tent. He was a foot from her face and almost didn't hear her. "No," he answered. "Couldn't."

He'd wanted to, had planned to take a phony shit break, but Sidney followed him and he ended up just pushing out a few sprinkles of piss. An emergency cry for help demanded privacy and Sidney was apt to follow him anywhere.

Renata held out her hand. "I'll try. I can say I'm pissing. Maybe they'll do the girl thing. If Sofia comes with me, I'll bash her face in."

"I don't know."

"It'll be fine."

From the other tent, voices were clearly audible, demanding they lower their whispers even further.

Raphael sighed. "Okay, but we wait a bit, you just got in here; they'll be suspicious."

Renata clucked her tongue once and then dropped to her side. Raphael dug into his pack for the portable propane campfire. It wasn't great—

being only eight inches high and four inches, cylinder tank included, he couldn't complain—and he hadn't bothered bringing it out until now, so it really hadn't been so bad until right then.

The flame rose from the canister with the power of about six candles, dancing gently with the exhalations of the pair. The tent was very small, and didn't hold heat very well, though was significantly better than being outdoors.

Renata smiled suddenly, looking down at the flame. "Remember that time the 'coon got into Mom and Dad's tent and Mom screamed and started beating it over the head with a flashlight."

Raphael said nothing for about a minute. "I hope to hell we're exaggerating the threat here; I mean they haven't done anything to us," he whispered. "We're only connecting dots."

"Then it'll be easy for us to make a call and get down the hill," Renata said.

"And what if it's worse than I'm thinking?"

Renata waited two seconds and decided she'd waited long enough. She snatched the satellite equipped cellphone and said at regular volume, "Gotta piss."

Almost instantly, Sofia said, "Me too!" The woman had very obviously been going down mentally as she had during every other tail of her high. Her words preceding taking to the tents had become self-deprecating while managing to be offensive toward both Riccardo and Sidney.

Renata tightened her fists within her pockets as she stepped around the snow they'd mounded. She began stomping a clear spot so her ass didn't get wet, waiting for Sofia, but the woman never came. Instead, footfalls crunched quickly down the hill until a weak cry rang out, followed by the sound of several thumps, each much further away than the last.

"Holy shit, she fell down the mountain," Renata said and then undid her pants and squatted. The light from the cellphone screen felt like a trouble beacon and she pointed it at her chilled knees.

More footfalls sounded, some very close by and some strangely far away.

Renata closed her eyes and begged the universe for a few minutes of privacy. She looked at the phone, it had loaded up, and she dialed the first number. That noise unique to telephones sounded and all the air left her. It was so loud, so obvious, so—

"Drop the phone, Sister," Sidney said. He had a rifle in hands; the barrel shined brightly beneath the moonlight. "Come on now."

Renata tossed the phone. Two zippers zipped almost in unison a second before the rifle barked and put a hole through the phone, killing the bright glow of the screen instantly.

"Renata?" Raphael said.

"I'm okay," she said, though her pants were around her knees and a man had a rifle pointed vaguely in her direction.

"How are we going to deal with you two?" Sidney said.

"Pretty close, could just pop'em both," Riccardo said, and then yawned. "Hey, where's Sofia?"

"We need them to help load the money." Sidney

was looking at Raphael with the rifle pointed at Renata still.

"She fell down the mountain. I heard her," Renata said.

"What?" Riccardo said and then closed his eyes. "Fucking junky."

"Guess you'd best go—"

Approaching footfalls silenced Sidney for a moment. A hooded head came into the sightline upon the ledge and then sleeved arms on a coat that was not Sofia's parka. Jenna Cashman's face arose like an unexpected phantom. Her expression was open and her eyes were stretched wide. Her cheeks had two large rough patches of windburn and her lips were scummy and cracked.

"You're real," she hissed.

"Who the hell?" Riccardo said, stopping.

"Jenna?" Renata said, unthinkingly straightening and pulling up her pants in a single practiced motion.

Sidney hadn't looked at Jenna. He also hadn't told Renata she could move. The rifle jerked as he put loose sites on her left boot. He fired and she fell back, began wailing as the shot's echo rang out over the landscape. He spun and aimed the rifle at Raphael.

"Take the bitch to your tent and stay in there. And you," he didn't turn or look at Jenna, but it was obvious he spoke to her, "you help them, since you're all acquainted. Riccardo, go find Sofia, if you're going."

Riccardo got moving again, stepping into his snowshoes before heading down the mountain.

"Me?" Jenna said.

"Is there somebody else here?" Sidney said.

"There's yetis," Jenna said, her voice low and her tone conspiratorial.

"Get outta here," Sidney said, smiling, though it was not a nice smile. "Move Sister into the tent with Brother."

Jenna clopped over, kicking wide strides with the stolen snowshoes. "There really are yetis; they ate Connor and Leon and I bet they'll eat that crazy man."

"Crazy man? Are you suggesting my friend Maurice is crazy, or that my friend Dusty is crazy?" Sidney said.

"Take off the shoes and hold her leg, don't touch her foot," Raphael said, laser focused on this one subject, despite the oddity around him. "Come on, hurry."

Jenna did as told and they lifted. Jenna was careful not to touch the injury, and even so, Renata groaned in pain as they moved her. Raphael hadn't closed the tent on his way out and only needed to mind the portable campfire. Renata came down gently at first and then Jenna stumbled and dropped the leg. The injured foot landed hard. An agonized growl rang long and loud from between Renata's clenched teeth. Sweat was heavy on her face and Raphael attempted to get his sister stretched out.

"I have to take your boot off. It's going to hurt," he said.

"Fucking just do it," Renata said, almost without ticks between words.

Riccardo then climbed back up onto the ledge.

"I don't see her," he said, not all that perturbed. "She can go hang with Maurice and Dusty."

"I do believe not making it to the top shall penalize their share," Sidney said.

"Sounds right to me," Riccardo said. "What'll we do about them?"

Renata screamed and blood poured out of her boot.

"Oh man. Hey, you got a phone, right? There's yetis, we have to get down to the lodge," Jenna said. "They're rabid, I think."

Raphael ignored her and tried to get all the pain over with as he didn't pause before dumping rubbing alcohol onto the wound. He lifted the portable campfire close for light and saw that the round had gone all the way through. Small favor. He packed and wrapped the wound and then held Renata tightly.

"So sweet," Sidney said, and Riccardo made kissy noises.

Raphael sat up and looked at Jenna. "Get in here, if you're getting in."

29

Sofia was off her feet and pitching forward, rolling and thumping, before she truly understood that she'd lost her balance. The itch for what Sidney had thrown away needed to be scratched, and not in the addict sense, or at least, that's not how she understood it. She had come down hard again, which did happen, and often, but she couldn't nurse her wounds on a fucking mountain. To get right physically, she had to be right mentally first. Meaning, she had to survive the mountain with her mind intact, and then worry about the come down.

Finally, after more than a dozen full revolutions, she wandered from the path they'd cut and landed face first in a mound of crunchy snow that scratched and cut her face, but ultimately gave her a soft enough landing that she hadn't done any worse than a sprained ankle and countless bruises. She gasped, sucking snow down her throat. Coughing came next. She rolled onto her back and stared at the moon a bajillion miles away.

In the time that she would've normally screamed, she was busy catching her breath and thusly remained quiet. Pain throbbed throughout and she recalled her task. She attempted to rise to her feet and instantly fell when the pain seared up her leg, as if she'd been sentenced at a witch trial and the executioner had lit his match.

The pain fleeted quickly and she looked up the mountain. She couldn't believe it. She must've fallen hundreds of feet, perhaps a thousand. Her eyes played back down the slope and only a yard from where she lay were two packets, still frozen together, shining in the moonlight amid a sea of sparkly snow.

"Thank you, God," she said and pushed to her hands and knees. She crawled quickly, but shakily, trying to keep from putting any pressure on the bum ankle. "Won't even hurt in a few minutes," she said then and reached for the packets.

30

He simply couldn't bring himself to do it and his mitten suggested that second-guessing was maybe a wise idea. Kevin reached one of his hovels. He lit a fire down inside a rocky, icy hole beneath him and let the heat cook from the feet up. He sat on a rocky lip within the hole and had his elbows perched on the ground beneath a pine tree. If he had to, he could duck down into the hole and wait out a few days—from his experience, yetis gave up sooner than later, but he still had the necessary essentials to survive in that particular hole. Not that he planned on drawing attention to himself.

He had his binoculars trained on the light about seven hundred feet up a fairly steep ascent. There was a closer hovel, but he'd have to pass the group to get there and since he'd fallen back on remaining an observer rather than participant in whatever was happening here, this was the best option.

"A buffet," he said and then heard a cry. He gasped, partly certain he'd blown his cover and that one of the yetis had clocked him.

But no. A woman tumbled by and stopped a little ways past him. She gasped and gagged and in the dark, thanks to the moonlight, Kevin saw this was a different woman from the one he'd trailed up the mountain.

She didn't move right away. Looked dead after the initial shock. Then she did move and when she tried to stand, she fell and shrieked in unison. Kevin nodded. Made sense she'd hurt herself, in fact, he was surprised she could move at all. The fall had looked downright cartoonish in its violence.

It wasn't long before the woman was crawling toward something, and around her, three humps moved in the snow, barely visible but for the long shadowy fingers dealt by the moonlight. Kevin held his breath. The woman reached for something and the adult male palmed her head like a basketball and wrenched it back. The snapping of vertebrae rang out like twisted bubble wrap. The adult female latched onto the woman's hips and pulled in the opposite direction. The neck tore in a splattery, bank bag spray—red rather than blue.

Things went their normal course then: the papa ate the brain, the mama dug through the entrails, and the baby chomped at what was offered. What the juvenile didn't notice, and what Kevin did not see, was that when a flank of muscle landed on Sofia's packets, those packets clung to the underside of the meat. The juvenile took that flank and chewed it down with enough amphetamines and coke to turn a temple of monks into whooping party animals.

Kevin watched without the binoculars. Anything for science of discovery. His belly told a tale and he huffed. His guts had begun bubbling and gargling, and were now falling through the coils of his intestines in a hurry to evacuate. He tried desperately to hold it, did not want to shit in one of his warmest hovels, but eventually ran out of options.

"Dammit," he whispered.

He'd lowered some and undid the belt around his pants, and then the fly. Living off canned meats and fruits, some power bars, some local Animalia, gave his digestive track all it could handle.

He gave up watching the feast and fell deeper into the hole. The fire filled the back third, while the middle third remained empty, and just inside the opening was a great stack of sticks and bark chunks. Panic was beginning to settle and he crouched into the middle of the smoky little space and tried to think of the best location to plant this particular bomb. Quickly thinking was off the table and his pants came down. He exploded against the sopping rock beneath him with a long, wet, clapping evacuation.

When it ended, he sighed and reached for snow from beneath the opening. As he grabbed a handful, the white fur and horrible claws of a yeti reached down. That shit had given him away. Above were growls and sniffing sounds. Kevin swiped the snow between his cheeks, neither bidet nor tissue, but instead something uncomfortable and in between.

His mitten seemed to say, "Now you dunnit."

"It's okay," he whispered, calming himself.

They'd stay interested for up to a day, and until then, he was stuck. But afterward, he could crawl out, and hell, they'd likely bugger off before then, given how much food was currently on the mountain. His pants came up and he dragged sticks from the big pile to beneath him so he could rest without sitting directly in the mess he'd made.

He'd huddle within his parka and for the coming hours feed the red hot embers a stick now and then, finding the comfiest space between breathable air and liveable temperature.

31

Before sunup, Raphael had removed everything from the sleigh, fastened his sister to it, and piled what they'd actually need of the removed items back on top of her. Jenna had ceased talking about yetis and was instead zoning out—she hadn't slept, the fingers of the drug still itching around her edges, even after the energy had depleted. Sidney had risen, as had his rifle. He looked downright ill, but also resolute. Riccardo rose only when ordered to do so by Sidney, otherwise, all remained quiet.

"Not taking your tent?" Sidney said.

"We get you to the top and then we turn around or you kill us, what do I need a tent for? Without you unskilled meatheads slowing me down, I could have Renata at the hospital by midnight," Raphael said and then took the first heavy steps up the final chunk of mountain, his sister strapped in and scowling at Sidney and Riccardo.

"Meatheads? Now that isn't very nice, is it, Ricky?" Sidney said, words dripping in faux outrage.

"Don't call me Ricky," Riccardo said. He was looking down the mountain at a strange dark splotch amid the sea of white—color unknown; the sun was still an idea lingering to the east. "What's that? Think it's Sofia?"

Sidney looked and the corners of his mouth down-turned. "Looks like a shadow to me."

Jenna leaned in close to the men. She'd gone a

little feral after the happenings she'd recently experienced. "It's her. Yetis ate her up," she said and then made a slurping noise. "They'll eat us all up."

"Move, you wack job bitch," Sidney said and shoved Jenna forward.

She walked slowly, slower than Raphael with the sleigh, but Sidney and Riccardo weren't about to catch her. They'd fallen to less than half the speed they'd been going up until then.

The sun came up and kept coming. At the noon hour, they hadn't reached the top, as the schedule had dictated until that morning. Wind battered them and nobody spoke, only Renata could see much of anything. With her hood up and back to the wind, she watched the struggle behind her, and distantly, watched peculiar movement. She shook her head and blinked. The snow wasn't thumping around, that was a trick of the light, or her eyes, or…something.

Raphael began creating more and more distance. Jenna flagged. Sidney flagged. Riccardo was way, way back. Two o'clock had hit and the lip at the edge of the peak had come into Raphael's view. The air was thinner and each step felt heavier, but they were almost there.

A huge mounded shape, grey beneath a thick blanket of snow, rose in the distance and Raphael paused. He then scanned the landscape. He'd been up here before, and knew there were caves, but didn't recall the exact layout. He wanted to tuck Renata away, but wasn't sure what use it would be. If Sidney used that rifle on him, he was about as good as cooked goose. Whatever they'd come up here for was beneath that lump of snow.

Raphael looked back down the mountain and did a bit of time guesstimation. Maybe ten minutes. He took a deep breath. He crested the final steps up and then started across the flat space in as close to a jog as was possible in snowshoes with a pack sleigh strapped to his back. The mound wasn't far.

He recognized the shape: a wing and the plane's hull. He could almost touch it. Old blood had crystalized within and enormous footprints rimmed with pink ice stood out starkly.

"Holy shit," Raphael said.

"What is it?" Renata said.

"Holy shit," Raphael said again, seeing two duffle bags zipped closed on the floor next to one with a tear in its end, revealing bundles of money.

"What? Talk to me," Renata said.

"I gotta…" Raphael trailed as he looked around. He needed the upper hand and there was a cavernous ice cave with many chambers up there, but which was it? There were three cave mouths. He grabbed the handles of the two zipped duffle bags and grunted as he hefted them out of the plane wreckage. He kicked around and set them on Renata's lap.

"What's this?" Renata said, the weight heavy, the contents less than solid.

"Cash," Raphael said and scoop-grabbed the torn duffle, which was less than half the weight. "It's why we're up here."

Renata's eyes bulged when she saw the bill bundles. Millions of Euros in her lap. It triggered a memory of something she'd read on her Twitter feed maybe a week prior. Someone had made off with more than €800,000,000 in cash from a securities warehouse after kidnapping and threatening someone's family. The robbers had set out multiple red herrings and so far, the authorities had no leads beyond that the crew were made up of East Coast Americans, the survivors saying they sounded like TV mobster types, but talked less and didn't dress like TV mobsters. Obviously, seeing it in these particular mountains, the cash had made it out of the country of origin, but not far.

"This is from…there's…" Renata became short of breath—all that money!

"I know," Raphael said and re-harnessed the sleigh to his back.

There'd be tracks to the cave he'd settled on, but there was no helping that, not with the limited time available. He went with the hint of a lingering memory and chose the cave mouth to the north. Once into the shadows, they immediately began ascending into the frosty gloom of the ancient ice chamber. The sleigh skated on the icy floor behind him as his mind rebuilt what he'd almost totally forgotten.

He'd selected correctly. This cave had a maze of nineteen interconnected chambers. Taking the correct paths all the way along would let them loop a route in and out, but that was too much to ask of his memory. He took off a mitt and pulled a penlight from his coat pocket, and then followed the blue and white wall until a right turn presented itself. He took it and did the same thing with the light, but took a left in the next cavern, and then another left. The hope was to get behind Sidney and his rifles and barrel down the mountain on his skis, the sleigh out front of him.

"I need you off there for a minute, trust me, okay?" Raphael said and bent to take off his snowshoes.

32

Kevin awakened cold and stiff. The shit smell was gone thanks to freezing and the yetis gone, likely thanks to boredom. He looked at his mitt. A smear of waste ruined the face he'd drawn and he was suddenly all alone.

"Oh no," he hissed.

He decided he couldn't live like this, not while he might yet have some survivors to corroborate his findings. He'd get down the mountain, tell of an emergency, and once the parties were in motion, he'd reveal the truth. He'd take a skilled team and a high-definition camera to all the important spots. He'd hunker down with that team and catch hours upon hours of footage. He'd make a documentary. He'd write books. And not only non-fiction, he'd pen monster books and sell the rights for movies, he'd be a millionaire.

He'd live among the people until the next cryptid demanded his undivided attention.

Kevin climbed from his hole and immediately had to stop. Not twenty feet away, the juvenile lay on its side, its breaths labored. Further up the mountain, he saw a dark figure cresting the top and another figure still a ways down. Not far from that second figure were two telltale humps of snow. They were stalking, but for some reason had left the juvenile behind.

Unable to help himself, Kevin took a step closer to the downed beast. Its expression seemed pained and both of its great hands rested between its thighs in a strangely human posture of sickness. Seeing it this way hit Kevin deep down and he moaned a gentle, "Aww."

The sound caused the beast to open its eyes. The irises were gone and its gums had stretched back while its tongue danced like rubber over its incredible teeth. Something very unusual was going on.

Kevin darted back in the direction of his hovel, but the juvenile popped to its feet as if this had all been planned.

"Oh," Kevin said when the yeti was suddenly between him and his safe space.

It roared and Kevin spun on his heels, thinking the next hovel was down the hill and through some deep snow, no more than three hundred feet away. It wasn't one he liked, as it was too cramped for comfort, but it would keep him safe.

After two steps, a shadow began passing over him like a blimp before thumping to the ground directly in his path. This was all new and strange behavior—he'd never seen a yeti jump even half that high. Something had changed, something had altered its mind.

"Okay," Kevin said and began backing up, holding eye contact.

The yeti leapt again, springing up as if playing leap frog. It sailed overhead, but landed much closer to Kevin than the first time. He spun and felt the hot, meaty breath of the beast on his face.

"No, up there. There's—Ahh!"

Kevin got only one step in reverse when the yeti

latched onto his head with both hands and tossed him into the air. He landed with a great thump and then a greater thump landed on his back, sending the oxygen from his lungs in a single, painful bark.

Feet on his shoulders, the yeti pulled at Kevin's head. He wailed, even after the skin tore. He wailed, even after his spinal column snapped midway. He wailed, even as his decapitated head looked down at his lifeless body and the massive pool of blood turning the snow pink. His wail trailed as the little beast played monkey see, monkey do and ran a claw around Kevin's cranium, working to release the brain. The brain came free, but the yeti didn't eat. As if enraged, it charged up the mountain, cutting the deep snow in a flurry of action, Kevin's brain clamped in its right hand.

33

Riccardo watched a moment as way ahead, through the cutting winds, Sidney crested the mountaintop. He sighed and got back to moving along. Snowshoeing was the absolute worst when sober. He had to stop again after five more steps. He swiped his mitten beneath his nose, sending his ski pole out before him in a whipping motion.

A growl left his lips, and then, as if in impossible echo, he heard that growl come back to him. He turned his head to look over his shoulder— a pleasant reprieve from the slashing of the wind. He scanned the snowy trail behind him; crystals whirling tails like dust clouds. All appeared as it should, and he was about to continue on, when he saw movement way down, below the ledge and last night's camp. Another growl rose above the winds.

His eyes remained focused distantly until two large lumps shifted much more closely. The one to his left seemed to turn and a bluish visage, almost like a gorilla's face, revealed itself.

"Dear, Mother Mary," Riccardo said and wasted no time second-guessing himself or what that woman had said.

Snow and a gorilla face—well that was simply a yeti. Didn't need to be a mathematician to put that together. He chased after Sidney's lead, wanting to yell, but no longer having the lungs for it. He needed that oxygen if he was going to get up, get to Sidney with the rifle. He took ten, twenty, thirty great strides.

"Yes," he hissed as the lip to the top came into view. "No," he hissed then as a heavy hand pressed down on the top of his head.

He swung blindly, stabbing over his shoulders with the sharp-ended ski poles. The hand reefed backward and tossed Riccardo like a potato sack. He slid on his back, his snowshoes grinding before him and taking hold so he didn't fall far and didn't flip. The two beasts converged and he took another pair of stabbing swings with his poles—one had been broken and was now more short range than long range, something like a dagger. The bigger of the pair led the charge, coming at Riccardo's right. He took another swing. The ski pole swatted the beast, like hitting it with a fly swatter. It put its great hands on his head just as the other beast attacked Riccardo's left side. He stabbed the broken pole down hard and the crunch was incredible.

For a moment, all motion and sound stopped but the whipping winds. The ski pole handle jutted from the beast's forehead, as if it had been sheathed there. Red blood began to spill down the ugly blue face, matting the white fur and sending steam into the air. The beast tipped sideways and spilled down the mountain on her side.

The big one inhaled deeply and then cried out a great siren of rage. Slobber and bits of chewed Sofia rained down on Riccardo before the beast refocused and put its great hands on either side of the man's head and squeezed. Riccardo screamed as hot black pain filled his body a half-second before the cranium popped off his skull and his brain slipped out; cartoon spinach from Popeye's can.

34

Sidney followed the trail to the plane and Jenna followed Sidney; both assumed Riccardo was somewhere right behind them. Sidney reached the plane and saw the blood, and almost as quickly, saw the duffle bag-sized holes where no snow had yet blown. Beneath one of the seats were bundles of Euros. He didn't bother touching them, he'd come back for them after he relocated the duffle bags.

He started away from the plane without a word to Jenna, following the clear path that trailed into one of the caves and chambering a round as he did so. Jenna watched him go and then looked at the wads of cash. The beauty of it stole her breath.

She'd never have to wait another table again. Suddenly energized, she began squirreling the cash into the many pockets of her coat. She'd collected €400,000 when an incredible cry rang out and reminded her of an impending demise at the hands of a trio of bloodthirsty beasts.

She bent to unlatch the straps from her stolen snowshoes, dropping a wad of bills in the process, but leaving them be; for now anyway. She scrambled up into the cockpit where blood stained the seats, floor, ceiling, and walls. The dash was crusty with pink crystals. She snatched up the microphone from behind the steering handles. She pressed the button and listened, then spoke. Pressed it twenty-nine times in quick succession, knowing the thing was dead. She huffed out a big steamy breath and surveyed the rest of the cabin. So many dials and meters, none of it looked helpful. She leaned to look under the co-pilot seat and found a strange red dome. There was a switch next to the dome with a toggle. A few words gave her hope: BEACON, ALARM, TEST. She flipped the toggle and a green light glowed. Almost non-existent, thin buttons sat atop the steel surface. They were perhaps two millimeters across. She stabbed a cold-chapped finger into the ALARM button. The green light turned red and began blinking, but nothing more.

Outside the plane, and coming at her fast, grunts and footfalls told her she had no time to play the wait and see game with the crash position indicator unit. She hopped into the co-pilot's seat after a quick glance out the windshield. The biggest of the trio was charging through the snow like a moose.

She gasped and ducked, checking for something, anything.

There was a tin first-aid box. She yanked it away, hoping something hid behind it. The lid opened as the box tilted, spilling the contents, including a bright red flare gun and two flares.

"Bingo," she said and went about loading a cartridge—thankfully it got no simpler than it was. As she rose to assess where the beast was, the plane rocked and the yeti wailed, thumping great dents into the steel hull. "Help!" she screamed, bouncing around the craft.

She fell between the pilot chairs and stumbled to the floor just in front of the first row of seating. The plane continued rocking and the semi-detached wing that had made it that far finally crunched, letting the hull roll onto its side.

Jenna was too rattled to gauge the beast's location or know the doorway was suddenly above her rather than behind her. A shadow fell over the plane and the beast reached in, snatching Jenna by the hood of her coat. She lifted, but slipped, almost coming free thanks to the bulkiness, but didn't because she clamped her arms at her sides, trying to keep from losing the cash she'd stashed. Yeti breath bathed her cold face in meat-stinking saliva as the beast roared before tossing her high into the air. She thumped into a crunchy cradle of snow and whooped, gasping for the air instantly forced from her lungs upon impact.

The beast was on her anew. Its claws dug into her skull, carving at meat and muscle. Blood rained down her face and neck. Her vision faded. Her gasps slowed. Just as her cranium popped, her body tensed and she inadvertently fired the flare into the beast's leg. It hopped away from the sudden pain of impact and the slower pain of the flare's flame catching onto its greasy fur. Flames began licking up the beast's legs as it stumbled in reverse, following the path carved toward the cave.

The flames reached the yeti's abdomen and panic set it. It turned and ran, as if to escape the flames. It growled and moaned and from the mouth of the cave, Sidney watched in amazement until amazement became fear. That flaming mass of creature was coming right for him. He aimed for the head and fired.

A fine mist blew out. The beast toppled

sideways and big breaths rose as it dropped; the pyre upon its body growing larger and more ravenous. Finally, the yeti whimpered and moaned for several seconds until it only burned.

"Jesus," Sidney said.

35

Sidney watched the yeti burn until the scent of charred fur got to his mouth. He spat. He unstrapped the snowshoes, eyes steady over his shoulders and on the hill, waiting for Riccardo to show, or Maurice, or Dusty even.

"Fuck'em," he said and clumsily shifted the rifle to his right arm while he bit off a mitten. In his left pocket, he had a flashlight; the quickly setting sun barely reached into the cave. "Fuck'em," he said again and stepped into the gloom. The flashlight beam lit and cut a wide cone through the darkness.

The icy floor was far from smooth and Sidney's boots found sufficient group to hold his balance as he waved the rifle and the flashlight. The realization that he might simply walk by the siblings was made obvious quickly. He needed to stir them. Scare them.

"Hey, where'd you go?" he said and waited, shuffling along, light banking off the blue and white walls and floor—a floor with some scoring, hopefully from a weighty sleigh. "I know you have my money. I don't want to hurt you, I just want my money."

Even as he said this, he knew they'd never buy it, but presenting himself in this way was the most reasonable thing he could think of.

He crossed the threshold into a secondary chamber and saw two options; both tunnels were dark and slim. He scanned the walls and floor.

"You know, when I shot you, I was a little out of sorts, nothing else. If you give me my money, I'll let you ski right on down the mountain, easy peasy lemon squeezy. Come out and everything will go smoothly, okay?"

Sidney stopped and listened. He heard nothing beyond the winds dancing across the doorway of the cave. He shined the beam over the floor and found the scores in the ice that he sought. He followed their trail into the next chamber.

"I'm starting to get annoyed here. You don't want to annoy me. Just come out with my money and I'll kill you quickly, no pain. If you make me trail you around, I'll do unspeakable things to both of you. You'll bleed. Your bones will snap. You have no idea how deep your fingernails run until they're pulled out. You have no idea how much I'll enjoy pulling them out."

Sidney stopped in another chamber; again, two options presented themselves. He almost laughed at how deeply the skis of the sleigh cut this time. Then he heard a voice, close, very close.

He shuffled quickly, trailing along the heavy marring of the icy floor.

36

Raphael had Renata and the money back on the sleigh just in time to hear Sidney follow the ruse he'd created by tipping the sleigh on its end and dragging the frame into the chamber next-door.

He had his skis on, back-tracking the way they'd come, pushing Renata and the money. The shush-shush of his skis seemed like a bullhorn.

"Sonofabitch!" Sidney shouted, distantly.

Raphael pushed as hard as he could, about to round the final corner before they'd again see the waning moments of daylight. A sound stopped him in his tracks. A growl followed by a high-pitched squeal.

"God," Renata said under her breath.

Raphael cut across the chamber to the deepest shadow available. There, he crouched. Behind them, Sidney was shouting that he'd kill them. That, "I'm gonna cut off your eyelids and make you watch me—sonofabitch!" His voice had risen and fell, as if he'd slipped. "Christ fucking bitch!"

The beast loped into the cave and looked around, seemed to spot Raphael and Renata, but Sidney shouted again, and the beast tore off. Raphael wasted not a second and pushed the sleigh to the door. Dusk had hit. The shoulder harness slipped into place. Behind them, several rifle shots barked off, one after the last.

"Go! Go!" Renata squeezed the bags, as if they'd somehow buy their way out of this trouble.

Raphael kicked and pulled, the sleigh sinking at first, but picking up speed when Renata used the snowshoes like paddles, lifting some of the weight from the back end with each plunge. The lip of the ledge was coming at them and suddenly it seemed they might just make it. Raphael got them onto the original trail then and going was fast, fast, fast.

"We're doing it," he said.

37

Sidney pushed to his ass after slipping. He winced at the pain. He'd managed to keep hold of the rifle, but the flashlight was several feet in front of him. "I'm going to do any old thing that comes to mind, I'm going to…" he trailed.

A yeti slid into the chamber, Tom Cruise *Risky Business*ing its entry. It roared. The flashlight beam squared on its hips, banking a campfire tale shine up its furry chest and to its wild eyes.

Sidney was not too shocked to act, despite being as shocked as he'd ever been—more shocked than when he walked into his parents' bedroom and saw a woman under his father who was not his mother; more shocked than when the 2007 Patriots shit the bed in the second half of the Super Bowl after a perfect season and playoffs. He fired. The rifle bucked and blood spurted from the beast. He fired and chambered. He fired and chambered. He fired. Each shot nailed the thing, but it kept coming.

"Die already," he said, chambering another round.

He fired again, and hit the target. The target had had enough and leapt, screaming a bestial war cry gone deranged on expensive dope. It thrashed and pounded, tearing and smashing. Blood ran and the yeti ripped and wrenched. Intestines flopped free. Ribs snapped. Muscles snicked away and slipped hotly across the glacial floor of the cave. Sharp teeth peeled flesh. Eyeballs gushed in the beast's mouth like grapes.

After three minutes of destruction, the pain of those shots finally struck and the urge to sit, the urge to rest for a little while was so strong the juvenile yeti nearly succumbed. But distantly, it heard a voice beyond the cave.

Fury pushed all else aside and the beast charged out and into the gloomy evening air. At the edge of the mountaintop, there they were. The beast fell to its fours and loped, zeroing, targeting; the intense need to destroy becoming everything in the world.

"Raph!" Renata shouted, seeing the shadowy figure racing toward them.

She tossed the snowshoes over her shoulders. The wind whipped them high and gone from sight. Raphael crested the hill at the same moment and the sleigh followed. He gave two strides, but the sleigh was twice his weight and took him out at the knees. Renata's hands wrapped around her brother's stomach as the sleigh bolted down the mountain.

Behind them, the beast cried out and it sounded as if they'd made some room between them. It ran as hard as its legs would carry it, but lost its footing and began tumbling, quickly making ground on the Le Pages, skipping like a stone.

Renata made a terrified humming noise. Raphael couldn't breathe; they were going too fast and even moving with the cutting wind, they were jarred going against the frosty atmosphere. They covered a day's hike in less than a minute and before they knew it, they'd hit the plateau atop the rocky outcropping. The edge jutted almost thirty feet on their current course.

Nothing but air beneath them, they soared over the deadly rocks while the juvenile yeti cartwheeled and bounced, too high to feel much of anything. They landed just before the rock face clipped off, nailing a slick of ice that had Raphael snap his jaws together tight enough to break all of his teeth. Renata kept humming. Higher than high, they began rolling sky tumbles. Renata's grip tight. The straps holding her and the cash to the sleigh just as tight.

They landed; Raphael's face came down on his arm and he broke his nose and wrist. Renata kept on humming. The beast bounced, still trying to focus on its prize, as if invincible. They were all on the final leg and though none of them saw it, they were about to hit the auxiliary parking lot behind Le Sommet.

38

Cody Desjardins was more than a little drunk as he backed the ice thrasher attached to the PTO shaft at the rear of the tractor, clearing the thick mess from the asphalt. The damned winter birds; they couldn't use salt at Le Sommet because the local birds ate it and swelled so fat they froze to death in front of the patrons. And some folks you just didn't let see dead birds lying around.

So, the ice thrasher. Slow going, it was like a snow blower, but it featured more than one thousand teeth on three rolling shafts that turned inches thick ice into tiny pellets. Indochine's *L'Aventurier* was on the tractor's stereo and Cody sang as he drove in reverse across the lot.

Raphael saw the back end of the thrasher and began to scream into the wind—no breath in his lungs be damned. Renata kept humming. Raphael leaned and Renata followed, bob-sledding, unknowingly shifting them far enough to ping off the side of the thrasher's mouth.

The yeti hit the level ground and found an upright footing, but skidded on its backside, kicking and swinging wildly, trying to slow its lightning pace. It hit the thrasher teeth square. Those teeth sucked the beast in, sending out a blood shower from the release hopper.

Cody howled over the beast's screams, "*Et soudain surgit face au vent!*"

39

Giving up the money stung something awful. It almost felt as if they'd earned it after making it down with the bags. On top of it all, Raphael needed all new teeth. Renata smiled at him and said, "I got you, bro."

"How?" he mumbled.

"Let's just say your sister planned ahead. I'm no millionaire, but it turns out my snow pants can reasonably conceal more than five hundred thousand without causing any concern," she said.

Raphael looked at her, squinting, then shrugged.

40

The plane's crash beacon could be switched off. Technology was usually good like that.

The same couldn't be said for the yetis' internal systems. From centuries before humanity invaded their space, they'd developed signals. A death of one of theirs tripped something deep and carnal within the families of yetis living in the mountains behind Le Sommet. Before anyone had come to collect the money and investigate the scene, beasts moved in quickly to collect corpses for burial. The mess of the juvenile was too far gone to retrieve.

Their survival relied on these evolutionary tools that they'd developed and their survival relied on remaining a myth. The yetis living on the mountains behind Le Sommet would remain, as would their taste for human flesh.

THE END

Check out other great

Cryptid Novels!

P.K. Hawkins

THE CRYPTID FILES

Fresh out of the academy with top marks, Agent Bradley Tennyson is expecting to have the pick of cases and investigations throughout the country. So he's shocked when instead he is assigned as the new partner to "The Crag," an agent well past his prime. He thinks the assignment is a punishment. It's anything but.Agent George Crag has been doing this job for far longer than most, and he knows what skeletons his bosses have in the closet and where the bodies are buried. He has pretty much free reign to pick his cases, and he knows exactly which one he wants to use to break in his new young partner: the disappearance and murder of a couple of college kids in a remote mountain town.Tennyson doesn't realize it, but Crag is about to introduce him to a world he never believed existed: The Cryptid Files, a world of strange monsters roaming in the night. Because these murders have been going on for a long time, and evidence is mounting that the murderer may just in fact be the legendary Bigfoot.

Gerry Griffiths

DOWN FROM BEAST MOUNTAIN

A beast with a grudge has come down from the mountain to terrorize the townsfolk of Porterville. The once sleepy town is suddenly wide awake. Sheriff Abel McGuire and game warden Grant Tanner frantically investigate one brutal slaying after another as they follow the blood trail they hope will eventually lead to the monstrous killer. But they better hurry and stop the carnage before the census taker has to come out and change the population sign on the edge of town to ZERO.

Check out other great
Cryptid Novels!

Ian Faulkner
CRYPTID

Be careful what you look for. You might just find it.1996. A group of 14 students walked into the trackless virgin forests of Graham Island, British Columbia for a three-day hike. They were never seen again. 2019. An American TV crew retrace those students' steps to attempt to solve a 23-year-old mystery.A disparate collection of characters arrives on the island. But all is not as it seems. Two of them carry dark secrets. Terrible knowledge that will mean death for some – but a fighting chance of survival for others. In the hidden depths of the forests – man is on the menu. Some mysteries should remain unsolved...

Eric S. Brown
LOCH NESS HORROR

The Order of the Eternal Light, a secret organization have foretold the end of the human race. In order to save all humanity, agents of the Order must locate the Loch Ness Monster and obtain a sample of its blood for within in it is the key to stopping the apocalypse but finding the monster will be no easy task.

Check out other great

Cryptid Novels!

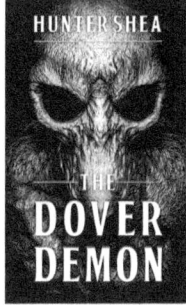

Hunter Shea

THE DOVER DEMON

The Dover Demon is real...and it has returned. In 1977, Sam Brogna and his friends came upon a terrifying, alien creature on a deserted country road. What they witnessed was so bizarre, so chilling, they swore their silence. But their lives were changed forever. Decades later, the town of Dover has been hit by a massive blizzard. Sam's son, Nicky, is drawn to search for the infamous cryptid, only to disappear into the bowels of a secret underground lair. The Dover Demon is far deadlier than anyone could have believed. And there are many of them. Can Sam and his reunited friends rescue Nicky and battle a race of creatures so powerful, so sinister, that history itself has been shaped by their secretive presence? "THE DOVER DEMON is Shea's most delightful and insidiously terrifying monster yet." – Shotgun Logic Reviews "An excellent horror novel and a strong standout in the UFO and cryptid subgenres." –Hellnotes "Non-stop action awaits those brave enough to dive into the small town of Dover, and if you're lucky, you won't see the Demon himself!" – The Scary Reviews PRAISE FOR SWAMP MONSTER MASSACRE "B-horror movie fans rejoice, Hunter Shea is here to bring you the ultimate tale of terror!" – Horror Novel Reviews "A nonstop thrill ride! I couldn't put this book down." – Cedar Hollow Horror Reviews

Armand Rosamilia

THE BEAST

The end of summer, 1986. With only a few days left until the new school year, twins Jeremy and Jack Schaffer are on very different paths. Jeremy is the geek, playing Dungeons & Dragons with friends Kathleen and Randy, while Jack is the jock, getting into trouble with his buddies. And then everything changes when neighbor Mister Higgins is killed by a wild animal in his yard. Was it a bear? There's something big lurking in the woods behind their New Jersey home.Will the police be able to solve the murder before more Middletown residents are ripped apart?

www.ingramcontent.com/pod-product-compliance
Lightning Source LLC
Chambersburg PA
CBHW051953170626
46808CB00007B/2603